Bright Island

Bright Island

Mabel L. Robinson
with decorations by Lynd Ward

A YEARLING BOOK

This is a work of fiction. Names, characters, places, and incidents either are the product of the author's imagination or are used fictitiously. Any resemblance to actual persons, living or dead, events, or locales is entirely coincidental.

Text copyright © 1937 by Random House, Inc., copyright renewed 1964 by Howell A. Inghram and George C. Thompson

Cover art copyright © 2012 by Dan Williams

Interior illustrations copyright © 1937 by Random House, Inc., copyright renewed 1964 by Random House, Inc.

Visit us on the Web! randomhouse.com/kids

Educators and librarians, for a variety of teaching tools, visit us at RHTeachersLibrarians.com

Library of Congress Cataloging-in-Publication Data
Robinson, Mabel Louise, 1874–1962.
Bright Island / Mabel L. Robinson ; Lynd Ward. — 75th anniversary ed.
p. cm.
Summary: When sixteen-year-old Thankful Curtis must leave Bright Island, Maine, for the first time in 1937, she has trouble adjusting to life on the mainland, new people, and "proper schooling," and yearns for her days of farming with her father and sailing.
ISBN 978-0-394-80986-1 (trade) — ISBN 978-0-394-90986-8 (lib. bdg.) — ISBN 978-0-375-97137-2 (ebook)
[1. Boarding schools—Fiction. 2. Schools—Fiction. 3. Interpersonal relations—Fiction. 4. City and town life—Maine—Fiction. 5. Coming of age—Fiction. 6. Islands—Maine—Fiction. 7. Maine—History—20th century—Fiction.] I. Ward, Lynd, 1905–1985, ill. II. Title.
PZ7.R5674Br 2012 [Fic]—dc23 2012009178

ISBN 978-0-375-97136-5 (pbk.)

Printed in the United States of America
10 9 8 7 6 5 4 3 2 1

First Yearling Edition 2012

Random House Children's Books supports the First Amendment and celebrates the right to read.

To Mildred, a valiant sailor
and
To Ruth, who sailed her into port and came back alone.

Contents

PART IV
BACK TO BRIGHT ISLAND

Bright Island

PART I

On Bright Island

Bright Island

Out where the quiet bay widened into the darker blue of the ocean, Bright Island lay quite alone. Its bay shore was curved into a smooth cove which caught sunsets on its yellow sand. It climbed toward the ocean end through pastures of sweet fern, lifting itself by boulders rougher and barer until it flung a headland of them out into the sea where the water was never still. Where the rocks reared highest some strange writhing of the earth had left a mass of gleaming white stone which held the sun all day. The lobstermen set their course by Bright Island.

The island was complete; cool woods, meadows of blowing hay for animals, and a weathered gray house on the sheltered bay. The hot July sun poured over its silver roof but the curtains blew out with the sharp breeze which ruffled the bay into shining fragments of light. Even without the wood smoke from the kitchen chimney the island had the air of a place where people lived. A faint cowbell, the bleat of a lamb, the neat rows of green potatoes, a lobster boat swinging at its mooring with Sunday idleness. The house had no neighbors but it seemed to need none.

The kitchen door opened with an energetic pull and a woman peered out at the bay under the shade of her hand. She saw what she evidently expected, a white sail in a slip of a boat just dipping out of sight around the point of the cove. "It mightn't be too much to expect," she reflected aloud, "if you have a girl that she should be some help on a day like this. Well, it will be something to be thankful for if she turns up at all." She tested her oven and slid two pans of trussed-up chickens on the hot grate. "Shouldn't have named her that, I suppose. Seems to set her to doing things that wouldn't make anyone thankful. Aye, but she can't be young but once," and she fell to thinking of her own young days as she pared the vegetables at the wooden sink. Six boys she had raised on this island, all grown but the two in the small graveyard fenced in from the sheep. She could see it from her kitchen window. Four fine boys left to her, all married and away on the mainland. They were all grown and well scared that night she was taken. She could remember the dream as if it happened last night of her painful toiling up the steep hill at home in Scotland, the one called Rest-And-Be-Thankful. Sharp stones cut her all the way and harsh winds buffeted her. But at the top the sun shone and the green hills of Scotland stretched away at her tired feet and she was suddenly filled with peace. When she came back to her senses and knew that the seventh baby was a girl she decided to rest and be thankful, and that should be the baby's name. Thankful they called her, and as there was no minister on the island for a christening only her mother knew her full name.

She was contented enough, this Scotch woman on a Maine island, and if the daughter wasn't turning out the sonsie buxom creature that she could expect of a Scotch lass, she had too many other concerns to worry about Thankful. In spite of her homesick dream of the home mountain she would rather live here than anywhere else in the world. She felt a queen in a well-ordered domain, well-ordered because she herself carried out her own orders. That was the kind of queen to be.

Today the sons and their wives were coming over from

the mainland for Sunday dinner. Mary Curtis would not have asked them at just this time when the berries were ripe and needing her care, but they had suggested it themselves. "Some kind of advice those girls think they should be giving us, it's likely," she speculated. "Well, it never does them any harm to give it." She made room for a big blueberry pie in the crowded oven. "Wonder if Jonathan found all his clean clothes. Oh, you did, didn't you?" to the man who looked so clean that she needed no answer. She got none. Jonathan usually let her answer her own questions. But he saw to it that his own were answered. "Where's Thankful?" he said.

Mary Curtis said she didn't know and it was quite obvious that she was more interested in the state of the chickens than in the location of Thankful. "Sunday's her day off from lessons," she offered, "and she's out in her boat somewhere. She's still missing Gramp, I guess."

"And could she not help her mother with eight people on the way to dinner?" Jonathan looked grimmer than Mary liked to see him.

"Here"—she took a clean tablecloth out of a drawer—"set the table with the best dishes. She'll be along soon. She didn't want to see them much anyway."

"Well, why wouldn't she?" Jonathan bent his lanky length over the table, smoothing the cloth with big painstaking fingers. "Her own brothers, ain't they?"

"Not all of 'em," chuckled his wife. "Don't forget the wives."

"Not likely to." Jonathan held the bitter conviction that these mainland girls had stolen his boys away from the island.

"Anyway," Mary comforted him, "the babies have to go to their other grandfolks. We'll have none of them under-foot." She liked children well enough but she had brought up her own and as far as grandchildren were concerned she was still determined to rest and be thankful. "Well, things are about ready. See if you can hear Jed's powerboat." She looked as unhurried and cool as if she had been sitting in her rocker all the morning. "Small need I have of help," she remarked to the empty room, "but the lass better get to the mooring before her brothers."

Again she shaded her eyes and looked out over the cove. The putt-putt of the motorboat was just around the point. The light breeze had died out and the bay lay flat and white in the noon sun. She shook her head. "Becalmed. Another good excuse for not getting here. Her father will be in a fury."

The sound grew louder and she reached for a towel to wave. The boys always expected this greeting. Then she began to laugh. The powerboat chugged into the bay tugging a small sailboat which still flaunted a useless sail. In the stern she could see the sun-bleached head of her daughter who held the tiller to the very mooring. "And who will be in a fury now?" She felt sorry for the child dragged home at the tail of a powerboat to a dinner which she hated, but there were the vegetables to dish up, and cold water to draw from the well. Thankful couldn't run wild all the time. She sighed a little herself for the quiet which would not be hers again until sundown.

It was soon gone, that peace which seemed to belong to the old gray house. It never had seemed overfull when the boys lived in it, Mary Curtis thought. It must be the wives. There seemed to be more than enough of them to go round. The girls chittered and chattered so. Thankful had disappeared again, her mother hoped to put on a clean dress. The girls fussed so over her overalls, even for sailing. Too bad they couldn't have found her at home all tidied up.

Everybody was offering to help, but Mary Curtis, moving competently among their protestations, had dinner on the table before their outstretched hands could seize a dish. Just as heads were bowed for grace Thankful slid into the only empty chair and ducked her pale mop of hair over her plate. In the first solemn moment after her father's Sunday prayer, all of the eyes, pairs and pairs of them, bored into her. Except mother who was testing the edge of the carving knife. Thankful met them fleetingly under the fine wings of dark eyebrows which gave her a startled look.

She stared at her plate again until she was sure that

food had taken their attention. Then she watched them speculatively with eyes that seemed to be measuring them up. Ethel, the big blonde, moved uneasily under the scrutiny. The rest watched the division of the white meat. Thankful had the kind of eyes that belong to lighthouse keepers and island dwellers, deep blue used to seeing quiet scenes as well as storms. The way they looked out under the dark winged eyebrows and the mop of hair bleached lighter than her sun-warmed skin made her what the girls called an odd-looking child. Ethel always said it was hardly decent that a girl as old as that should wear so few clothes but perhaps she spoke out of an envy for the long light body they failed to cover suitably. Thankful looked fragile but no one knew better than Ethel, who had once tried to discipline her, how false an impression she gave. Thankful came of strong stock.

The boys looked it, hard-muscled all of them except Homer who had softened in his clerk's job. His father eyed him contemptuously. Though Homer was his mother's boy, not his. They had alternated in naming the boys, and Jonathan's boys were like their names, rough and plain. Jed, the oldest, owned a powerboat which supplied lobsters to the big fish markets. Silas, the third boy, was fire warden on the mountain though his wife and children spent most of their time with her folks at the foot of it.

Mary Curtis chose her names from the books she had studied and taught in the days in Scotland before she had come to America. And both her boys had indoor jobs. Homer, the clerk in the town bank, and Petrarch, who owned his grocery store and ran it with profit. Among them all Thankful had early learned the art of dodging and disappearing. They seldom caught her as they had today. It was the wind, she thought resentfully.

The wives Thankful scarcely bothered to keep separate. They looked alike and talked alike and acted alike. She wondered how the brothers had ever selected them. She knew how steadily they were trying to make her alike, too, and learned a different kind of dodging. "It's as hard to put your finger on her," Ethel said, "as if she was greased lightning. I hope no child of mine will take after her." But so far she had seen no signs.

"Seems kinda queer not to be hollering at old Gramp." Gladys poured gravy over her potato. "He was getting pretty hard to talk to."

Thankful's eyes flew to the little fenced-in graveyard with its big new mound. She almost expected Gramp to come in and settle Gladys for that remark. Didn't the silly idiot know that the reason he was hard to talk to was because he wouldn't listen to her emptiness? And all he had to do was to shoot one glance at Gladys under those black eyebrows, and didn't she squinch up! It was like a clan when Gramp sat there erect at the head of the long table with Jed, the oldest boy, on one side and Thankful, the youngest girl, on the other. He ruled his clan well, that old sea captain, and Thankful thought she would never be through missing him.

Out of all the strong boys the girl was his favorite, the only one of them that cared for the sea. Thankful looked at her father bent with the tasks of the land and saw him through Gramp's eyes. She could hear him telling how he had sent his boy, Jonathan, to sea only to have him sick all the way across, and back with a schoolteacher wife he had picked up in Glasgow, and a set against the sea that no one could alter. "But an island is next best to the ship," she could hear him say, "and this one has always belonged to us and always will, please God."

He had suffered when the boys, one by one, took up their lives on the mainland. "And where will Bright Island go next?" he would ask. "There's only you, my girl, that can abide it."

"I would live nowhere else," Thankful would promise him. "I will marry a sea captain and when we have sailed all over the world we will settle here and have ten children, all sailors." Gramp would laugh, but he liked to hear her say it.

He had built her a boat and cut the sail and sewed it. She had helped, and they rubbed it down and polished it like a piece of rare old furniture. He had cut the letter patterns for the name, *Thankful*, and one day when he was busy she had taken those she could use and cut others until when he came back he found painted on the stern in letters that slid a bit, *The Gramp*. She could still hear him roaring at her, but he let them stay.

Thankful sighed softly and listened to voices nearer. Jed was talking to her and she liked him best. "And what would you think of that, old Corn-tossel?" he was asking. He grinned at her puzzled face. "Haven't heard a word of it all, I'll bet."

Gladys interrupted his good-natured protest. "I should think she might at least listen when we take the pains to plan things for her."

Thankful was still so close to Gramp that she wanted to reply in his words, "Who asked you, and who wants you, to plan for me?" She didn't know how exactly like him she looked out under her dark brows at Gladys, but she noticed her startled blink. Gladys did not interrupt Jed again.

"Time you had some real schooling, we think." *We* means the girls, Thankful thought scornfully. "All of us boys had to go over to mainland High long before this. Of course"—he nodded respectfully toward his mother—"of course she knows how to teach you and you'll learn more Latin and Algebra than you'll ever need. But we think . . ." He hesitated.

"We think," finished his wife, "that a little wholesome life with other young people would do you no harm." She looked around the table for support.

To Thankful's faint dismay they all seemed to be giving it to her. But after all, she thought, they're not my father and mother. "I have my lessons every morning, don't I, mother?" she offered.

"Certainly do," responded Mrs. Curtis briskly. "A good learner, too. Got all the Latin I know."

"That's just it," Sadie leaped in, "she's got to stop because there's no one to teach her any more."

"At that," said her husband dryly, "she knows more than you, my girl."

Thankful flashed him a grateful glance. Sadie had the air of settling with Silas later.

Jed went on with patience but as if he wished someone else would undertake the job. "You could take turns staying with us, except Silas, of course, on top of the mountain." Only place I would stay, Thankful thought, if I was silly enough to stay anywhere but here. "Pete has a nice little car to take you over to school in bad weather. And there's the movies twice a week. And church socials, and—and . . ." His voice trailed away under the blank unresponsiveness of Thankful's face. "Well," he said cheerily, "what do you think of the idea?"

Thankful felt about in her mind for something satisfactory and found nothing. "Thank you, Jed, and the rest of you"—her eyes touched the circle of faces pressing in on her—"it would be very nice. Especially the mountain." There, she didn't mean to say that! "But I like it here. And I wouldn't think of bothering you. And mother's a good teacher. And well—I guess I'll stay here. Thank you." Now that was settled. She drew a long breath and wondered how soon she could get away from the table. Her gull, Limpy, was yelling for his dinner out there on the *Gramp* where she had left him so that he wouldn't hop on the dinner table. And her goat was scrapping with Rosy, the lamb, who teased him and could take ample care of herself, and the breeze had come up again and was flapping her sail which she hadn't stopped to furl, and altogether what was the use of wasting any more time here? The girls always washed the dishes.

"'Scuse me, please," she muttered, and pushed back her chair.

"Wouldn't go just yet, Thankful." Surprisingly enough her mother had taken a hand. "Might as well settle this thing."

"I did," murmured Thankful poised on the edge of the chair.

"Well, I wouldn't say settled," her mother said judiciously. "After all, your father and I have got something to say about it." The girls nodded vigorously. "I don't know why these young people should want to add to their work by taking in an outsider"—("Oh, no, mother Curtis, one of the family!")—"but since they have offered we'd better think it over. Sit right down, Thankful."

Thankful sat down dazedly and looked at her father. He would certainly have no hand in this outrage. He stared thoughtfully out of the window. Her eyes followed his to the quiet graveyard. He knows what Gramp would have told them, she thought hotly. And it wouldn't have been Sunday talk either! They wait until he's out of the way before they try any of their tillie-vallie. The Scotch had words for things, as the children of Mary Curtis knew. Thankful watched her father's gaze draw slowly back into the room and toward her. Now he would tell them, though not exactly in Gramp's words, Thankful grinned, the way that Gramp would have settled such nonsense.

The smile altered into tight-lipped listening. Could she believe her ears? What was he saying, her father who almost never said anything? She had never felt near to him, like Gramp, but these slow final words were pushing her away—away from everybody—she moved her head from side to side, and they were all against her. What was he saying!

"It would be a very good thing for her. She's run a bit wild on the island. But now father's gone"—was he blaming her Gramp because she had been so happy with him?—"'bout time I guess that she found out what a girl's for." He spoke like a judge, impersonally. Thankful thought wildly, Who'll help me now? Who can I go to? "School won't be beginning for quite a while and I guess we can get her fixed up before September. What say, mother?"

"Without a doot." Mary Curtis rose briskly to get

15

the berry pie. Thankful saw her chance and slipped out behind her mother. She heard her say, "Just give her a chance to get used to the idea and she'll take to it like a trout to a burn," and then the girl ran—ran as if the whole clan was after her. Even in her haste she did not forget to seize the gull's dish of scraps. An upside-down world did not necessarily mean a hungry gull.

The outgoing tide had left the dinghy high up on the beach. Thankful rushed it down into the water with such blind force that the waves splashed over the stern on the seat. She shoved the boat off with an oar and pulled herself with short furious strokes out to the *Gramp*. She flung herself aboard and made the dinghy fast to the mooring. "Clean dress ruined," she noted, and pulled a pair of blue overalls, sprayed with dried salt, from the tiny cabin. The lame gull who had screamed from the moment she left the shore dug his head into the dish of scraps. Thankful cast off and slid down behind the tiller. The boat shot silently out of the cove into the sparkling outside water.

The gull finished his scraps with noisy gulps and waddled over to the stern coaming where he could reach down and pull Thankful's hair. She obeyed his demand for attention by absently rubbing his smooth feathers. After a while he clambered out to the bow where he perched like a figurehead drenched with spray. Sailing was next to flying.

Thankful sailed on. Sailing was better than flying. You sat still and the clean water poured around you, and the sweet air washed you clean. No one could reach you. You were safe—for a while. Why couldn't she get away from them all in her boat? Stock it up and slip away some bright day. And go on sailing and sailing, she and Limpy. He would like it, too. But Thankful was a sea captain's granddaughter and she could not fool herself about the sea. Bright weather did not last, and neither did food. And a powerboat would soon drag her home again as it had this morning. This terrible day that had started out so gaily! The sunlit head went down on the tiller.

But sails flap when they get no attention and, in spite of herself, Thankful had to watch the freshening breeze. Before long it did its work, stiffening her as it did the sails, pulling her erect and alert. The lee rail was where she liked it now, well under water. She stood braced against the tiller, the spray dashing salt mouthfuls into her face. The gull dipped and flapped his wet wings to keep his balance in the bow. Bright Island was far astern, its gleaming peak picking it out of the dark blue. Before long all those people would be gone and the island would be itself again, hers to live on as long as she pleased. And that would be forever. Her spirits lifted like the gull's wings. Let them try to catch her, let them try to catch her. She whistled and sang and called to Limpy who found her more companionable now and hopped back to the stern to perch on her shoulder.

Let them try to catch her, the song went all right until

the *Gramp* finally had to go about and head in for home. Then it died out a bit and finally as the sun slid down behind the purple mountain there was no song at all. Thankful shivered though not from the quick cold that came with the north twilight. The gull was chilly and had huddled himself into the sheltered cockpit. Thankful made a long tack and rounded the point of the cove. She knew that Jed's boat with its noisy passengers would have gone long ago, but she still felt a quick lift of heart at the empty bay. The *Gramp* slipped back to its mooring silently, just enough breeze left from sundown to take it home.

By the time Thankful had her sail furled and the boat made shipshape for the night, yellow lights sprang from the kitchen windows. She picked up the sleepy Limpy who protested with ruffled wings, and dropped him into the dinghy. She rowed slowly this time, dipping her oars into the stars as she went. The gray peace of the house with the darkening sky bending over it soothed her fears. They could not take her away from Bright Island. It was her home.

What's a Girl For?

Through the night her father's words troubled her between her dreams. She would lie there in the cool dark listening to the faint splash of the incoming tide, half awake, half asleep, and suddenly she would hear her father's voice instead of the touch of the water on the beach. Time she found out what a girl's for. Sleep would not come then though usually she drifted off to the sound of the tide as if she were on her boat. Time she found out what a girl's for.

It wasn't so hard to know what he meant. She ought to like to cook, and dust, and sew—she knew. She had heard him tell Gramp what he thought and had known only careless delight in the argument because Gramp's word was the final one. His strong arm fended the others away from her, and left her free. She turned uneasily and stared out at the stars. Now she must fend for herself. And against so many!

Toward morning she woke to a sense that partial surrender would be easier than complete. She made a sleepy vow and did not stir again until her father's heavy step tramped down the narrow stair. The day had begun and she must make it count. For a moment she considered saving the time of her early swim, a crazy thing to do anyway, the girls said. Imagine jumping into that icy water first thing in the morning! Enough to make your heart leap right up into your head! Thankful reached for her scrap of wool sweater sewed up into a sort of suit. Things that the girls said were crazy could not be omitted. She would hurry.

She raced through the kitchen where her mother lifted an amazed face from the fire she was laying in the stove. Out into the island morning. Aware all at once that mornings could never feel like this, clean and cold, except on islands. Unbreathed air! How could the boys leave it for the thick smell of the mainland? A whitethroat whistled at her.

The water was cold, and it did make her heart leap, leap so that she sang as she poised on the tip of the high rock for a final plunge. Her body curved like a young moon and down she went to touch the sandy bottom of the cove. A moment to float with her face so close to the surface that the ripples closed her eyes. Then the swift hard crawl to the shore. Now the morning was well started no matter what the process of learning to be a girl meant.

Helping to get breakfast, it meant first. Her mother seemed to be getting along very well without her and when Thankful offered to fry the bacon and eggs, said that it had taken her quite a while to find out just how a man liked them and, deftly turning a golden egg, perhaps she'd better keep on. Thankful could see how that was, and she set the table. Her body felt cool and light and she moved swiftly back and forth into the dining room. No, she wouldn't get along without her morning swim.

She skimmed the cream from a yellow-filmed pan in the cellarway and put the pitcher by her father's porridge dish. One thing Mary Curtis had taught her family was that it was no breakfast without the good start of a dish of porridge. She stirred the cream down into her own tall glass of milk which was always set aside for her at the night's milking. She poured her father's great cup of coffee from the pot on the stove, and rang the bell for

21

breakfast. She felt that she was doing very well indeed. Jonathan paid little attention to her. Haying had begun and there was no one to cut it but himself. He missed his boys most in the haying season. It had been a matter of no moment when he had those strong arms to help him. Thankful liked the work in the hayfield but she made her reluctant hands collect the pile of breakfast dishes, eggy, greasy—and hay was so warm and sweet! She whirled at her father's voice, "I'll need you in the field today. Sunday's made a hole in my work. You can spread while I cut."

Off with the gingham dress, on with the overalls, out into the sunny field when she had thought of the day shut into kitchen walls. She would do the work of ten boys! Yet, Thankful jammed the prongs of her pitchfork into the stubble and leaned against it, was this learning what a girl's for? Oh, well, it was her father's own choice and who was she to find it faulty? Tomorrow she could try a bit of cooking but today he certainly needed her to pitch hay.

All day she worked in the golden sunshine. The gull hopped about behind her, croaking at the prick of the sharp stubble and urging her to notice the fresh sailing breeze. But Thankful was content enough. When her arms ached she flung herself into a fragrant pile and shut her eyes against the sun which made glowing patterns on her lids. Over in the cool green of the spruces a hermit thrush sang, infinitely lovely. She listened to the notes deepen, lift, lift again, and thought no wonder the hermit chose to sing when all birds were silent.

At noon another swift plunge which quickened her wet body into fresh vigor, a prodigious dinner, and then back into the fields until the shadows grew long across them. That was the way to spend a day, she thought drowsily over her supper, even if it had all been on the land. She liked working for Bright Island.

Sleepily she heard her father telling her mother how much *we* had done, and that this weather wouldn't last, the wind had turned southerly, that haze meant a fog out to sea, and then a rough jerk back into sharp awareness of her mother's, "Well, and good, but who wished her more womanish in her ways? Does a hayfield help to soften a lass?"

Jonathan grumbled uncomfortably and pushed back his chair. "She'll soften fast enough on the mainland. Let her go to bed. She's near asleep now. It's been a hard day." And he stumbled out to the porch and his pipe, taking her drowsiness with him. What could she do to please? What could she do? He would send her away because of the very work which helped him most. But the sun, and the wind, and the steady tossing of the hay had done something to her bewildered mind. It would not think, it would not feel, it would only sink down into the feather softness and dark of sleep. Thankful did not stir her straight and quiet length all through the night.

The rooster crowed and crowed before Thankful heard him. She staggered like a sleepwalker down the beach and threw herself into the least cold-looking wave. The shock left no sleep in her tingling body. She leaped out of the water quicker than she had gone into it. Storm coming, she thought, and fog. Feels as if it had already got here! I can smell it coming!

The sun had no cloud near it but Thankful did not need her father to tell her that the rest of the hay must go into the barn today. No question was raised about what she was to do that morning. In her overalls she hurried through a breakfast which her mother put before her as she served her father. Two eggs, a slice of home-cured ham, fried potatoes . . ."

"You eat like a hired man," her mother said.

"Am as good as one," returned Thankful but she stopped eating at once when her father pushed back his chair.

They walked down to the barn together, the lean stooped man and the tall light-limbed girl. She looked as good as a hired man except for her mop of hair. Her father didn't seem to mind having her along, she thought. She buckled the harness under the tired sagging belly of old Sparrow who got his name no one knew where unless it was from his dun color. Sparrow hated to start but he knew what Jonathan expected of him. His hoofs pounded out of the shadowy barn into the blazing sun, reluctant to

stand in the heat all day and to drag the heavy overhanging loads of hay which was much better eaten on the spot.
Thankful curled up in the empty rick and knew how he
was feeling.

Down the rutted track to the outer fields where the cut
hay had lain longest. The cart swayed and bumped over
the imbedded rocks that no man would ever try to smooth
away. Almost to the headland that reached east into the
sea. When Sparrow stopped, Thankful saw between the
side rails of the cart the wide stretch of shining ocean.
Nothing between us and Spain, her father often said.
Nothing this morning except a whitish soft band of extra
light which meant the fog was waiting for the tide to turn
and bear it in to the land. Even in the hayfield she could
hear the slash—slash—of the ocean rollers rushed into
the gashed rocks by the sea wind.

Whether it was the haste impelled by that pale threat
outside, or tired muscles, or the cussedness of things as
Jonathan himself said, Jonathan managed to get his foot
under Sparrow's stupid hoof. No bones were broken, he
could tell by moving them, and he saw no reason why
he should not go on pitching hay into the second load.
But he leaned against the cart after each forkful, and then
Thankful saw the queer color of his skin, gray under the
mahogany. It was time for something to be done.

He was easier to manage than she had expected. He
sat up in the hay rubbing his foot and looking as if he

would like to kill Sparrow. Thankful drove the old horse who went quite willingly in this direction. A small flock of sheep grazed across his path and scattered with silly bleats when Jonathan shouted at them. "Be stepping on them next," he muttered.

"You've done it now," Thankful informed Sparrow from her perch above his tail. "Walk yourself into that barn."

Thankful saw her mother anxious, a surprising state to her. But Mrs. Curtis examined the foot rapidly and lifted a reassured face. "Keep off it a couple of days and I'll have it as good as new with my bottle of arnica."

"And what about my hay, just ripe for the mow? As good as new that will be," responded Jonathan sourly. "It's a pity I have no sons!"

Thankful sat hunched on the driver's seat, her chin in her hands. Now's my chance, she thought. If I could get that old hay stored away, he'd think I was some good. She looked at her mother for a suggestion but her mother was urging and pulling her father toward his chair on the porch. What's hay to her, thought Thankful, or what becomes of me either. I can't get that heavy stuff in alone.

She sat there while Sparrow comfortably munched the dried clover from the stanchions. No use trying to get one of the boys. They were busy as minks about their own affairs. What's hay to them either, she thought. I know, I'll get Dave Allen. He'd rather make hay than can blueberries any day. I can get him in the noon hour!

She leaped from the cart over to the porch almost in one long motion. "I could sail across to the factory wharf in no time." She measured the wind along with Jonathan. A sail! A sail! After two days!

"Aye, and have to beat back," came unexpectedly from her mother.

"Take the powerboat, if you must go," said Jonathan grudgingly, "and crank her with care. We want no broken arm as well as a broken foot."

"It's no break, and she can run the boat as well as you can," she heard her mother reassure him as she raced down to her dinghy. After all a boat's a boat even if it's a powerboat, she thought. Limpy was there before her, scuttling along over the beach to reach a place in the dinghy before she could catch him. "He's as dry as I am, the poor haymaker," she said. "I'll soak you down well. Get up there in the bow." The gull was content.

Thankful had to roll up the wheel three times before it caught. "Watching me from the porch doesn't help," she groaned from her knees as it finally fired. She had cast off first, and the onshore wind nearly had her aground. She could see that Jonathan wasn't taking care of his foot now—he was perched like a stork on one leg as tense as a string. Thankful rounded out of the cove with a wide flourish.

The trip was easy and swift. Dave was just beginning

his lunch on the wharf, lounging in a group of men, most of them young like himself. Thankful cared little for them though they tossed scraps from their lunch to her gull. In her overalls she felt like one of them rather than of the giggling girls across the wharf. "Can you come, Dave?" She went directly to the point. "There's hay to be made."

"Sure." Dave tossed a crust over the edge of the wharf and Thankful caught the gull as he would have plunged for it. "Not yet, my lad," and she reached for a handier piece of bread from the boys. "Just wait till I get my time." Dave disappeared in the factory.

"Go on, let me run her over." Dave sprang after Thankful as she shoved off with a boat hook. "Haven't had my hand on a wheel for longer'n I could count."

"Neither've I." Thankful believed it. "But you can start her if you want," she conceded. She wouldn't care to try three times with that audience on the wharf.

Dave rolled her up with one mighty swirl and slouched down into the stern. Out of his lunch box he took an immense sandwich which Thankful's hunger could not endure. "Want one?" he asked. Thankful took its mate and passed the wheel over to Dave. You had to make some concessions.

"Tell you what. I'll eat half your lunch and then I won't have to waste any time eating after we land."

"What's your rush?" Dave seemed to think very little of her idea. "You seem awful busy all at once."

"Well, now"—Thankful broke the third sandwich in two and gave Dave half—"I am. And so'll you be before you know it. You'll be staying to supper anyway"—this sandwich had blackberry jam in it!—"and if we get hungry before then I'll get us a snack."

Dave looked doubtful, but it was something to have the wheel. He bit into his final half. "Gosh, I'll be glad to eat on the island again! Remember the strawberry shortcake your mother used to make us when we picked her enough field berries? Was that good, or was that good!"

"We might have a raspberry shortcake tonight." Because of the possibility, Thankful divided a piece of apple pie and ate her half. "I saw mother out berrying yesterday when we were haying."

Dave's brow cleared entirely. "Say, I'm glad you sent for me! But how'd you happen to? More hay than usual?"

"About the same"—the lunch box would never be emptier—"but silly old Sparrow plunked his foot down on father's."

Dave looked concerned. "Hurt him?"

"What do you think? Sparrow's got a hoof like an elephant anyway. But it didn't break anything, no thanks to him. And here was the hay waiting to be put in, and you can see for yourself what's waiting outside." She pointed toward the band at the horizon which had broadened and grayed, and moved in.

Dave sniffed the air. "Funny how quick you know the

weather as soon as you get outside. Say, too bad about your pa. But we'll get the hay in all right before dark. Watch us!"

Thankful hadn't had a doubt but what they would when she went for Dave. That year after his mother died when he had lived on the island with them, he had been a better worker than any one of the boys though he was younger. For this reason and others intangible but real, they had shut him out of their clan of four and leagued against him and Thankful. Even then, Thankful had a dory with a triangle of a sail and she and Dave never missed the boys if the wind was fair. It was harder in the winter but the younger pair grew unco smart, as Mary Curtis said, in taking care of themselves. She seldom had to interfere.

For four years Dave had been back with his father and stepmother. With no boat of his own he seldom got to the island now. "Oh, say," Thankful suddenly remembered, "when you going to take your seaman's exams?"

Dave cast a worried look at her. "Lord, Thankful! I'd rather be drowned than take those. I can sail a boat all right, but it's one thing to have her on the water and another on paper. Gee, I hate learning things out of books when they belong outdoors. Don't you?"

"I don't have to," Thankful began gaily but suddenly something dropped like a plummet in the region of her heart. It was things outdoors which had displaced entirely that dread of learning things out of books. She thought of telling Dave about the absurd and terrifying proposition but it needed time and she had to catch the mooring.

"Haven't forgotten how to bring her up," boasted Dave. "Gosh, if I could do the tricky things with a pen that I can do with a boat!" He sighed, and unaccountably Thankful sighed too. But perhaps Dave could help her out—he'd done it many a time before. They pulled up the dinghy and Dave rowed ashore as if his arms were swinging to some music of his own.

Jonathan was on the porch watching the cove and then the sky. He had no regrets that they would not come in for lunch and cast dark glances at Mary Curtis because she made them wait for a basket of food for a snack later in the afternoon. His directions to Dave were as peremptory and curt as if the boy had been one of his sons. Dave listened as he had learned to listen in the year on the island.

But when the two had dashed away from the gloom of the porch into the barn for Sparrow, out with the rattly cart, up into the head of the island noisy now with the roar of the incoming tide, they might have been off for a holiday. Thankful perched on the high seat with the reins in her hands, but Dave did the real driving from the road where he ran beside old Sparrow who felt it was no holiday at all and would have liked to step on Dave's urgent feet. The sun had the soft waiting look which they knew meant no wait at all for them. They flung themselves into action when the cart stopped at the outer field where Jonathan had left it.

At four they were well past the middle of the island, and the fog was no longer a threat. It was blowing in white wisps down the island, catching on Thankful's hair in fine drops which turned it to silver. No time for the sandwiches. No time for the talk that had been spattering back and forth, news of the island for Dave, of the mainland for Thankful. The holiday had turned into work which strained their tired muscles, silenced any attention away from it. At five when the last great load staggered under the barn roof already loaded to its eaves, a gust of rain drove after them to announce the end of the day's work. Thankful stretched flat on the fragrant heap which she had brought in and stared at the shadowy cobwebbed roof. "I wouldn't move," she said, "even if you stuck the pitchfork into me."

She could hear Dave still in action somewhere down below her, the thump of the wagon thills on the floor as he unharnessed, the dragging steps of Sparrow into his stall, his crunch of oats, a—and then the cobwebs closed down over her eyes and she slept in the sudden way of a tired puppy.

"Hi!" The fork was actually prodding her. "Your pa says leave this load in the wagon as long as it's under cover."

Thankful blinked over the edge of the hay into Dave's

eyes, their pupils black in the darkening barn. "Quit," she muttered, "I'm dead!"

The eyes approached, the fork grew urgent. "Raspberry shortcake! I smell it clear out here!"

"Oh, well." Thankful sat up and shook the hay from her hair. "Oh, well." She slid toward the edge of the hay and prepared to leap.

Dave jumped back from the wagon wheel where he was perched and caught her as she avalanched toward him through the cloud of loose hay. He shook her and stood her up. "What you trying to do? Join the porch hospital? Have some sense!"

Thankful twisted away from him, suddenly awake. She glowered up at him. "When I need you to teach me sense—" then she laughed. "Hungry. That's what's the matter with us. Let's get washed up," and they walked companionably toward the house.

The kitchen was warm with a heavenly smell of fresh shortcake. Mary Curtis had foreseen the need of an early supper when the shadows darkened the sky. The table was set by the kitchen windows as it always was when they were alone. An extra plate was the only change for Dave.

"Thankful!" Her mother's voice was sharply exasperated. "You're not taking a swim this time of night!"

The girl had dashed through the kitchen before she had finished. "Quickest way to clean up," she sounded halfway down the beach.

Dave shivered. "I wouldn't go into that water. . . . What are girls made of!" He took a pitcher of hot water from the stove and went over to the kitchen sink. Before he had rinsed away the suds, Thankful was back, swift with vitality which she drew from the sea.

"And hungry! Am I hungry! Oh, mother, am I hungry!" She was upstairs in long wet leaps.

"Waste no time talking about it!" But Mary Curtis never held an irritation. "Come on, now," to Jonathan who limped over from his rocker, "supper has to be early for the hired men!"

They ate, steadily, quietly, ravenously, through the platter of pink slices of ham, the heaped dish of creamed potatoes, the warmed-up greens, until Mary Curtis would give them no more. "I'll not have my shortcake wasted!" She removed the emptied plates and reached into the oven for the flaky cake which was no cake and was no bread but a crisp thing bred of the best in the two. She split it deftly, watched by eyes still hungry, buttered it, and poured over it a great bowlful of sweet red raspberries. "A corner piece for each of you"—she dealt them out—"and an extra bowl of berries for juice. There now, Dave, put yourself through that!"

Dave crunched the first forkful and not a word from him until his spoon had scraped the last drop of red juice. "Well, I don't mind." His plate pushed out toward Mary Curtis's silent offer. "I'm one up on you, Thankful." For

Thankful was indeed done, eyes closing, head nodding over the empty plate. It had been a day!

"Well," Dave sounded reluctant to move, "guess you'll have to wake up, Thankful, and ferry me home. Kinda thick out." He peered hopefully through the kitchen window dim with fog. "Better move right along if you're to get back before night."

"Not thinking of having you go." Mrs. Curtis rose briskly. "I'll get sheets on your bed and you can turn into it any time you want. She'd go to sleep at the tiller, and you'd do the same, so where'd you land? She can take you over early, right to the factory dock."

Dave tried to look as if he hadn't thought of the idea. He ducked his head with a shy, "So long since I've seen you folks. Like to stay if wouldn't make too much work."

"Work? Who's worked today?" Jonathan's voice was almost genial. He touched a match to the birch logs laid in the sitting room fireplace and picked up the *Bangor Daily News* which Dave had brought over. "You'll be seeing more of one of the family soon. Thankful's going over to school in the fall."

The words were said. After these days of silence, and of work which made her indispensable, Thankful had shut the thoughts of Sunday out of her mind. But she could not shut them out of the minds of these other people who had planned her doom. They were still ready to say that she must go. The incredible sinking as the frightened little thoughts leaped out of captivity! Couldn't Dave see her despair? It must be the firelight that made him look so glad. Dave never would rejoice over her fall. He leaned forward to look at her as if he could not believe his ears.

"Honest, Thankful? Honest? Are you coming over? To stay all winter? Oh, gosh, how *swell*! Where you going to stay?"

Thankful answered him with stiff lips and miserable eyes. "Too tired to talk about it. Father'll tell you. Guess I'll go to bed." When she lighted her kerosene lamp the flame blurred and danced. "G'night."

"Leave by six thirty," Dave called after her. And then she heard his eager, "When's she going? Where's she going to live?"

"Careful, lass." She had nearly collided with her mother on the stairs. "Watch the lamp! What's the hurry?"

"Tired. Going to bed." Let her mother go on down and tell Dave all about it.

"Tut, tut. And Dave here so seldom. I suppose the morning will be here soon enough for you. Your room's thick with fog. But that's the way you like it." She was at the foot of the stairs now. "I'll call you in time."

The sheets on her bed under the window were damp with fog, the pillowcase cold with it. Her mind was blurred again with fatigue but it held to a sense that something inevitable had happened. It believed now what it refused to believe before. She was filled with fury at her helplessness. "Worked so hard"—she stared at the gray squares of window—"and what good did it do? Might as well have let the hay rot in the field. Maybe better since he just wants to learn what a girl's for." She heard Dave stump wearily up to his old room under the eaves. "He's just as bad as the rest of 'em. Wait till I get him in the morning."

Some small comfort seemed to come from the idea of punishing Dave. He was the only one she could reach. She tried to put her mind on making him miserable instead of on those casual words of her father's which had so stricken her. And with no sense of stepping over the borderline of sleep, she was dreaming that she and Dave were sailing before the wind and as the boat rushed with incredible swiftness through the water Dave explained that he was taking her where she could learn what a girl's for. Curiously she seemed not to dread it either. She half woke, wondering why it had seemed so bad and slept again before she knew.

In the Fog and Rain

Thankful struggled out of sleep at her mother's call from the foot of the stairs. She could hear Dave moving around already. She lifted her head to look at the weather and sank back with a moan. Even the back of her neck was lame! It was still raining but the fog had lifted a little. No chance of taking the *Gramp* out in this! And Dave would be sure to want to run the powerboat. Well, let him. She wouldn't care if she never ran anything. She pulled herself up and thought of a swim with nothing but distaste. "I wouldn't go into that water, nothing could drag me down there. . . ." She sprang to the window and peered out at the astounding sight of Dave headed for the water with limping haste. A whirlwind of speed and she was beside him. They tore into the water side by side, gasped, groaned, flung themselves into the long swift crawl of the old days and raced across the cove. Out again and up to the house, their wet brown bodies dashing through the rain as if they had never known weariness.

"What possessed you, Dave?" Mrs. Curtis fried him another egg, and pushed the platter of ham toward him.

Dave grinned a little shamefacedly at the egg but took it. "Couldn't let her get ahead of me, could I?"

"Certainly not," said Thankful smugly, "not a chance."

Her mother looked at her suspiciously but said nothing. It was something to have her out of last night's mood.

There was a rush at the last to get the powerboat bailed and off in the rain. It always sputtered on rainy days. Dave said it wouldn't do to be late after taking the afternoon off and he pushed the old boat for all it was worth. In their long yellow slickers and oilskin hats they huddled together in the stern. The gull dipped enjoyably at the bow. It was not a cold rain and nobody seemed to mind it much.

As soon as they were well under way Dave began.

"Now see here"—he turned his tanned wet face toward hers—"let's hear all about this school business. You'd think I wasn't interested."

Thankful felt something lurch in her. Just when she found a chance to forget it a moment he had to bring it up. "There's nothing to hear," she muttered, "and anyway you heard it all last night."

Dave looked hurt. For a while he steered in silence staring at the compass in front of him. "Say, what's the matter with you?" he burst out abruptly. "Anyone would think you didn't want to go!"

The queer sick feeling burned away under her hot anger. She glowered under her dark brows into his startled face. "Perhaps you can think of some good reason why I should want to go. Perhaps you think it would be fun to go boarding around with those girls! You know how they boss! You know I'd hate it! You ought to know, but you don't know anything. You don't know anything!" Under the visor of her sou'wester her eyes looked almost black.

"Well, well." Curiously enough Dave seemed reassured. "So it's the girls. Well, they're all right, but I don't know as I would want to live with 'em. But after all it would be kinda nice," he finished lamely, "I could see you now and then."

"What's now and then?" demanded Thankful. "You've lived on the island a year and you know something about it. Did you want to leave it? No, you didn't. Watch that compass!" And Dave looked hastily away from eyes suddenly filled with tears.

The dock rose out of the mist and Dave made a quick change of speed. The jerk was unexpected to the gull balanced on the bow and he flopped down into the water. Dave made a sweep to avoid running him down just as the whistle of the factory blew. Thankful leaped to her feet and seized the wheel. "All right," she sang out, "I'll put you ashore and come back for him. He likes to float!"

Dave made the dock with a long leap from the deck. Thankful moved at low speed past it and left him. Bad's the rest, she thought. You'd think he might understand. She paid no attention to the wave of his cap. Where's that gull?

She did well to ask. Her gull was suddenly one of a thousand because a barrel of high-smelling herring ends had been dumped. They were all eating, ducking, diving; they were all gray and silver; they were all screaming.

"If I nose among them they'll all fly but Limpy. Then I'll fish him out." She crept into the swirling wings. They rose around her with a sound of tearing silk. All of them. Not one neat gray back left floating for her to pick up. Now what?

Had they killed her lame gull because he couldn't fly? Just in the minutes she had left him? There was no broken body floating as far as she could see into the mist. Wild things were cruel to each other. She had lived among them long enough to know. When she had dragged him from a rock on the headland in the spring he was nearly dead. And now what had finished him?

The fog was thickening with the tide. A fury of rushing wings wove in and out of it. The gulls could wait no longer for her to go. They settled all around her, clacking, fighting, swallowing anything in sight. Thankful felt a little sick while she searched. Great gray and white birds, with now and then a dark one, but alike, all alike.

The fog had shut even the dock and canning factory behind its curtain leaving her alone with the screaming gulls. She turned off the motor and drifted among them calling Limpy's name. And not one gull turned its beautiful head. She shook his empty dish over the swarming water, but what was that as a treat? Would any gull leave dead herring for the sound of an empty dish?

When the boat had floated outside their greedy zone, she rolled up the wheel. "Can't move faster than a crawl through this weather. Might as well start. Take hours." She watched over her shoulder as the boat crept away. Almost instantly the gleaming dip of their bodies was clouded by the fog, lost except for the muffled screams.

"Gone," she said aloud, "gone just when I needed him most," and turned to see him balancing like a figurehead on the bow. Even when she squinted her eyes, he was still there. When she spoke to him he paid no attention. He bulged a little as if well fed. He was all ready to be taken home.

"You know what," Thankful speculated, "that gull can fly as well as I can." She ignored him as an imposter and by and by he hopped down the deck and pulled her hair. She stroked his wet feathers and they forgave each other. "Dave did dump him off," admitted Thankful. "He didn't know he could fly again until he had to. Well, catch me lugging him round anymore."

She watched her compass with steady eyes and crept through dark rain-shattered water toward an island she could not see. Now and then she blew an old fish horn, but nothing else was stirring on a morning like this. The slicker kept her warm and she liked the rain in her face. The gull cooled off a bit from his adventure and she covered him with an old poncho. He went to sleep. "Hard morning, my lad," she said.

When the noon whistle of the factory sounded like a faint foghorn miles out, she chugged into the cove. "Not an inch out of the way, straight's a cable. Better'n Dave could do with all his pilot's exams."

Limpy stretched his head out of the poncho. Thankful paid no attention to him. She fastened the spray hood down to keep the rain out and pulled the dinghy, afloat inside and out, to the edge of the powerboat. "Come on, you fake, get in there." Limpy rolled his head up and looked at her. "All right, stay here." She stepped over the edge, watching him, slipped on the wet seat, balanced wildly, and went down like a plummet. The clumsy slicker

43

held her under longer than she liked but she knew how to fight deep water. When she came up Limpy was screaming like a banshee and fluttering back and forth from the boat to the dinghy.

"Best have done that first," she choked at him. "Hey, give me room to get off this slicker."

She held the boat with one hand and pulled out of the heavy coat with the other. It wouldn't do to lose it. She hoisted it aboard and then could pull herself after it. "Now, sir," she said fiercely, "you get over here into this dinghy."

Limpy had settled on the deck of the big boat. He did not move. Thankful was cold now, and hungry. She reached over and picked up the great bird. When she set him down on the wet seat, she slapped his long wet wings. He flapped them gently away from her.

Dinner was hot on the table. "Must be raining harder than I thought," said Mary Curtis, mildly surprised at the trail of water left on her kitchen floor.

"Is," said Thankful and went for dry clothes. After all she often had two swims in a day.

She rubbed herself down with a hard rough towel. Even her young circulation was slowed by this chill. "Dave's fault. He knocked Limpy off. Would be dry as a bone if it hadn't been for Dave." Then as the blood glowed warm under her skin, she grudged him a point, "Well, I guess I am anyhow. And I do feel pretty good!"

She looked as if she felt just that way, setting her room to rapid rights. The water darkened her hair and fitted it like a cap to her head. She ran her fingers through it to dry it and it broke into rough tendrils pale on the ends. She was not unlike a fawn, tawny-coated, swift, dark-lidded. Long and lean with health.

Her father was back in his rocker, dinner finished. His foot was nearly well, but there was no outside work to call him out in the rain. "Gone a long time," he remarked.

Thankful nodded, too hungry for explanations.

"Dave late?"

She shook her head.

"Like it over there?"

Thankful shot him a surprised glance. "I didn't land. Just let Dave off at the wharf."

"Be nice when you can stay over there and get acquainted."

Thankful did not answer.

"Won't it?"

"No, it won't," she said. She looked with distaste at her plate.

"Now let her alone," soothed Mary Curtis, "she needs a good dinner." She heaped some hot golden carrots on the slice of pot roast. It smelled good. Thankful bent a glowering look under her brows at her father who stirred uneasily. His father had too often looked at him that way. She ate silently and resentfully.

Her mother had the dishes washed when she took hers to the kitchen. She handed Thankful a dish towel. "Don't mind your father," she advised, "he only wants what's best for you."

"Well," said Thankful, "how's he know what's best for me?"

"He's your father, isn't he?" asked her mother reasonably.

Thankful wondered what that had to do with it. "Anyway," she said hotly, "Gramp never would send me over there to live with those girls. He couldn't stand 'em!"

"Tut, tut!" But Mary Curtis looked curiously troubled. "He was an old man. He couldn't know what a young girl ought to do."

He was the only one who did know, Thankful thought drearily, and he wasn't here to help her.

"Such a wet day we might as well redd up the attic." Mrs. Curtis wrung out her dishcloth and hung it over the stove. "Most time to dry herbs and not a inch of space to spread them. Want to help?"

Thankful followed her mother up the narrow stairs to the garret under the roof. The rain drummed steadily on the shingles so close to her head. A roof is good, she thought, remembering the sea. The kitchen underneath had warmed the air, and light enough filtered in through *the small end windows and the skylight. A pleasant place* for a rainy day. Thankful carried down armsful of old newspapers and odds and ends which her mother saved for a year and then cleaned out ruthlessly. When she went through the kitchen it seemed to belong to another life down there where things were used all the time. It still smelled of fresh baked cookies and Thankful ate one, leaning against the table where they cooled.

When Mary Curtis was satisfied that she had room to dry her herbs, she sat down on a broken rocker and folded her hands. "Try it on now," she said. "You may have grown to it this year."

Thankful opened the small leather trunk in the low corner and brought out to the light a sheet-wrapped bundle. She laid it on the old spool bed and folded back the sheet. The bright tartan plaid spilled through her fingers in the dark attic. She held the Highland suit up to her experimentally, and nodded. "I've grown to it," she said and stripped off her dress.

She stood a moment in her knickers like a tall boy while her mother watched, inscrutable. Then she was a real boy, Scotch, in kilts which settled above her bare knees as they should. After years of dragging up from ankles like a little old lady's skirts.

"Yes, you've grown to it," said Mary Curtis, and she sighed.

Thankful dove for the cap and set it down into hair so unused to captivity that it flew up instantly around the edges. "Now I hope I've not forgot the Highland Fling."

She had not. The boys had taught it to her when she was five. The loose boards shook under her light feet and Mary Curtis looked suddenly tired. "Well, that joukery-poukery is over. You looked like Robbie." She went downstairs to get supper.

Thankful called after her, "Is it mine now?" and bent over the dark stairwell to hear the faint impatient, "Oh, aye. You're grown to it." Thankful strode up and down the creaking boards, fingers on imaginary pipes, pleats swirling against her legs. It would be something to be a Highlander. Robbie must have hated to die. She sat on the edge of the spool bed and thought about it. And then she looked at her legs, straight and strong, and felt how she had grown so suddenly into this suit of his. He was sixteen, she thought, and now his suit is mine.

She took it off slowly and put on her girl's dress which felt loose and light. Then she hung the kilt over her arm and took it down to her room. It should not be wrapped up again. Unless—until—her heart squeezed itself into a little hard knot. She refused to think about going off, but she couldn't prevent a flashlight of Ethel's sitting room crowded with things and people. There was no place for her, no place. And here was her complete world. She hung the kilt in her closet, patted it absently, and went downstairs.

Holding the Summer Captive

Thankful thought that she had never seen a summer go so fast. There was no August at all! That long slow month which usually crept by, windless, with a pale flat sea only fit for a motorboat, became suddenly a time to shackle and hold. Better to drift with a flapping sail than to scud under a September wind this year. She tried ignoring the calendar for a while, thinking to lighten the shadow of each passing day. But then the date would leap black from the newspaper which she thrust under her driftwood fire, and her shocked sense that three more days were gone would turn her beach supper into a dreary rite. She discovered that her mind had a relentless way of refusing to dodge the truth. You can't live on an island, she thought sadly, and fool yourself about much of anything.

She put her calendar back on the wall then, and decided to fill each day of it so full that it would count as two. She was out in the morning as soon as the sky began to pale over the still, dark sea. She watched the moon grow old until one morning it was silver thread in the clear amber of dawn. I've seen the new moon a'borning, she thought, and put the lovely thing away to take out later when—ah, what could she do with young moons in those noisy crowded rooms over on the mainland. From Bright Island, high in the sunrise light, she looked across at it lying still dark and huddled under the mountain.

But another long day was hers and she would waste none of it. She had given up trying to prove to her father that she knew how to do a girl's work. Little good it had done her to spend those days puttering around the house under her mother's feet! The decision had already been made with a kind of solid agreement which included everybody but her. It would have slivered into fragments under one swift thrust from Gramp. But Gramp was not here. And she could not beat down that front alone.

Thankful was torn among the many things she wanted to do before a day closed. A breeze, and she and the gull were off down the bay until, as so often happened in August, the wind died down and she rowed the *Gramp* wearily home at twilight. A thick quiet day, and she disappeared into the mist toward the south side of the island where blueberries were ripening. Where it was so still that the berries dropping into the pail were loud, she crouched among the bushes stripping them by handfuls. She let the berries run through her fingers liking their velvety bloom. And she took fine care to cover each pail as it filled because Limpy's great bill had a way of helping itself. Mary Curtis said that she had never had so much fruit for canning in her life.

She said, too, when Thankful gave less and less time to her meals, even omitting them when it served her purpose, that there was no sense in getting all ramfeezled like this! After all, the world wasn't coming to an end this summer, and there'd be plenty of time even if you took some of it for eating and sleeping. But Thankful did not agree with her about the end of the world. She saw it coming on the fifteenth of September. And she meant not to leave an empty moment before that time.

Her father, curiously enough, seemed more concerned about her than her mother. Thankful was aware of his scrutiny during her brief intervals at the table, or while he was behind the *Bangor Daily News* which he read under the lamp these shortening days instead of on the porch. She moved restlessly away from any prying into the dread which haunted her. Outdoors again, where nothing looked at her but the stars. "Can't she stay still a minute?" she could hear her father's testy voice through the open window. "Oh, let her walk it off," would come her mother's comfortable response. "She'll chitter like a finch as soon as she has lived with the girls awhile."

"If I never do any more talking than Sparrow does," Thankful vowed, "I'll not chitter like those girls." Somehow the thought of living around with them had made of school such a lesser dread that she scarcely thought about it. Books were easy things to master if they could be made to take their proper place in the world. Mary Curtis had a light touch with learning which left odd, sometimes gay, but never dull impressions behind it. Thankful had rather a shrewd grasp of the relative importance of events and facts. But with people she had had small experience and of those who had come her way, Gramp had proved the only wholly satisfactory one. She had no wish to learn more of them. Especially now when Bright Island was making so many last demands upon her.

But she was not to escape them so easily. "The girls are getting your things ready for you," her mother informed her casually. "I knew you'd have nothing to do with clothes yourself, and I've no time to see to them. They'll be over next Sunday with some frocks to try on you. And you're not to glour and glunch over them, either."

Thankful looked at her mother under dark brows. "Or at me, either," Mary Curtis added. "I'll need some blackberries for a blackberry dowdy. There ought to be good ones left up at the old quarry."

Thankful reached for a pail in the shed and fled. Her mother looked after her commiseratingly. "Too bad to fash herself like that for naught," she said, and fell to scrutinizing a braided rug for moth holes.

The one place on the whole island which Thankful disliked was the old quarry. She never went there if she could possibly avoid it. She thought over all the other blackberry locations and knew that only in the sheltered gloom of the quarry would there be any berries left now. She climbed slowly up the slope past the little enclosed graveyard toward Quarry Hill. When had she been there before? Not since her goat, a frisky kid, had marooned himself on a rock in the pool and called her with plaintive bleats. Even the gull turned back today when he saw where she was going. She pushed on alone.

Just around the quarry the spruces had grown tall and thick since the days when men came over for granite for their foundations. It was years since those great solid slabs had been placed under houses, there to stand when fire and age had razed the wood above them. Huge blocks tilted into the black lake which had filled the heart of the quarry and made it look as prehistoric, Thankful thought, as the pictures her mother had shown her of Stonehenge.

Thankful knew, though, that her fear of the place went back to nothing more prehistoric than the time when she was four and fell into the deep pool from one of those very slabs of granite. She could recall without any difficulty how she had strangled down there in the black cold water, slashing her tender flesh against the rough stone as she struggled to pull herself out. Silas had heard her cry as he had been picking blackberries and had pulled her out and shaken her until her teeth chattered with shock and cold. She knew now that most of his fury was terror because she had been in his charge and he had nearly lost her forever. But although the years had gone by, and every inch of Bright Island had become dear, she still avoided the quarry.

She sat now at the edge of the pool and stared down into it. Somehow its blackness and threat suited her mood. Swallows, purple dark in its mirror, swooped and dipped into it. She was thinking so hard that she did not hear her father until he stood there under a tall spruce. He was looking at her in a queer startled way, and she rose instantly with her berry pails. "I'm getting blackberries," she explained and started toward the clearing.

"Sit down, my girl," he said, "there's no hurry," and he slouched down on one of the boulders himself.

"Mother wants berries for a dowdy for the girls."

Thankful's voice was stiff with embarrassment and rage at his discovery of her. She held her head high, hoping that her lashes were not wet.

"She'll wait." He motioned her to a rock near him. But then he seemed to have nothing to say.

Thankful leaned against a boulder, her head turned away from him. The tops of spruces stirred in a sea wind and then were silent. Her fingers twitched at the handle of her pail. She felt her father's scrutiny.

He spoke at last as if it were not easy for him. "What you doing up here, Thankful? Thought you didn't like the quarry."

His voice sounded worried, and when she glanced at him his eyes looked anxious. Thankful sighed. Did people really think that you would tell them what you were thinking about? "Just cooling off after the climb," she offered. "Guess I'm ready to pick now."

Silence again. Thankful's quick motion to leave startled her father into speech again. "You—you don't want to go to school, eh?" he felt his way awkwardly.

Thankful considered. There was nothing to lose now, no matter what she said. "It's not the school so much. It's the girls, living with the girls." She tried to keep her voice even.

Her father passed this off with, "Good for you to see folks."

Thankful's thin veneer of control disappeared and resentment boiled over. She looked at her father under deep brows. "Gramp would never have made me go," she said.

Her father moved uneasily as he always did when she looked at him that way. But he was ready for her. "Wrong," he said, "it was your Gramp who said you were to go."

Thankful felt as if a last support had pulled out from under her and that she was slipping into a pool as sinister as the one beneath her. Gramp, her Gramp, was reaching back from where he had gone to do this thing to her. She might have faced it with the knowledge that he was with her to support her. But now . . . "Did he"—her voice was thin—"did he tell you that he wanted me to stay with the girls?" He couldn't, he couldn't, she thought, when we felt the same way about them. She still bent her unwavering look on her father.

He stirred the deep mat of spruce needles with a twig. "Well, not exactly." Her heart lifted a little. "You see, it's this way. If you're going to make such a fuss"—he was resentful now—"you might as well decide for yourself. Your Gramp left a sum of money for your schooling. Quite a sum," he went on cautiously, "enough to last you a good long time if you didn't spend it all at once. Seemed sense to take the girls' offer and go over to public school where it cost nothing but your board to them." He stopped. "Can't you have sense?"

Thankful hurried him on. "Not if I can have anything else. What is it I'm to decide?"

"Spend it all now on the Academy," he snapped, "or save it for a rainy day."

Thankful stood up, straight and tall. "I'll take it now," she said. "Maybe it won't rain!" And when she walked out through the gloom of the woods into the sunshine, she felt as if it never would.

Her father stared after her, and then looked down into the black water. "Her mother'll think I'm crazy," he muttered, "but I guess nobody could hold out against the two of them. They always had things their own way when he was alive."

Out in the clearing the gull sat with folded wings waiting for her. "Come on," she cried, "let's have a fight!" It was their old battle cry that had not challenged him for weeks. He lifted his great wings and dashed at the arm she held out to him. She flung him off with a wide sweep. He fluttered in the sunshine and swept back at her. Off and back again instantly! She suddenly discovered that now she was no match for him. So strong and swift had he become in these last few weeks that the victory was his. She sank down into the tough meadow grass breathless with laughter, and rolled over just in time to escape a tweak at her hair. The junipers pricked at her and filled her hair with their pungent scent.

"Don't tell me you limped way up here," she said. "You waited until I was out of sight and then you flew like a regular gull. Limpy, are you getting ready to go away, too?" And all at once going away seemed to be the thing for gulls and girls to do. She lay still in a kind of peaceful torpor after the strain, and let the warm sun shine through her closed lids. Finally she sat up. "Thanks, Gramp," she said aloud. And fell to picking blackberries with such rapidity that Limpy realized the game was up and settled back on his tail to preen his feathers. A song sparrow scolded halfheartedly at him, caring little because her brood had flown.

Mary Curtis accepted the change of plans as Thankful's responsibility, not hers. "I wouldn't have decided that way myself. Seems too bad to let all that money go out of the family," she said judiciously, "but then you're only half Scotch. Though 'twas your father's idea, not mine. You must take after your Gramp, not us. Well," she added cryptically, "perhaps you've no call to fash yourself about the future anyway. Oh, aye, I'll tell the girls when they come over."

Thankful wondered fleetingly what she meant, but felt nothing but gratitude for her offer to face the girls. "It might be better," she said, "to wait until after I tried the clothes on." Her mother caught the glint in her eye and sent it back to her. "I'll do that," she agreed.

The dinner with the girls was a thing not to be dreaded. They were detached from her now. She could think with a kind of ecstasy of the future when she would not have to live with them. She felt quiet inside, resting

something which was very tired. Soon she would begin to
see some of the new hurdles waiting for her, but not yet.
Only the lazy peace of one problem solved.

"Would you wish to see some of the Academy cata-
logues?" Mary Curtis held out three of them to her as she
sat dreaming on the doorstep. "Found them in the drawer
of Gramp's workbench."

Thankful reached for them. Why did he have three?
And then she saw that they bore the dates of the past
three years. For as long as that Gramp had been planning
her future when he should leave her! Her eyes stung. She
opened the catalogue blindly at the calendar page. In a
minute she felt better. The school did not open until the
first day of October! Here were two whole weeks handed
out to her as another gift. She felt as if a fog which had
been shutting her in closer and closer had moved away to
a wider horizon. "Another two weeks," she told herself,
"and I'll probably not mind leaving Bright Island at all."
But she knew she would.

The rest of the catalogue left her dazed. She was still
trying to find out what it meant beyond bringing sheets
and towels when she heard the distant putt-putt of Jed's
powerboat. She flew to her room to brush some kind of
order into her mop of hair. Stockings, too, she decided,
and a clean gingham dress. She ran downstairs just as the
platoon marched into the kitchen, Gladys leading them
with a last year's Blair Academy catalogue in her hand.

"Found this on the steps," she announced. "For goodness' sake don't let her read about that highfalutin' place." She passed the book to Mary Curtis. "Put ideas in her head."

Thankful's horror lasted only an instant. Just means they'll argle-bargle about it all through dinner, she thought, there isn't a thing they can do. They were looking at her as if they expected her to say something. Well, she would. This was, after all, her job, not her mother's.

She reached for the catalogue. "I was trying to get some ideas out of it," she explained, "because I'm going there."

Now it was out! Mary Curtis looked pleased. Her father scowled and led the way into the dining room.

It was a good dinner and Thankful enjoyed it more than most food shared with the whole family. She sat very quiet, her eyes out of the window where Gramp was, while she thought things over with him. Once she smiled at his trenchant comment as Gladys had flung a bitter inquiry at her. Gladys was so annoyed that it seemed best to pay attention to her for a while. After all what was an hour when she had been released for the whole year! Gladys remained irritated. But somehow nothing that she, or the other girls who hated to see the board money go elsewhere, could say seemed to penetrate Thankful's remote civility. She had suddenly acquired immunity against them.

Even with the gift of two extra weeks, Thankful

could not bear to stay indoors today when the first gold of September made the bay shine. Her boat tugged at its moorings with the expectant gull tilting on the bowsprit. Though how he got out there without flying, she thought, the fraud! But the clothes waited to be tried on. Without any glouring or glunching, either! You had to have clothes no matter where you went, away from Bright Island.

The girls found satisfaction in delaying the time when they needed Thankful, though her mother suggested that they leave the dishes until the clothes were settled. No, they said, we must not feel rushed. The lovely day slipped by while they did this and that, and Thankful mourned at its passing. Days were shorter now, much shorter.

At last the women all went upstairs to Thankful's room where the bed was covered with boxes. She followed them, head bent, feeling all soft inside from dread. Clothes, even one at a time, made her unhappy. And now she must twist and turn for them to stare and comment. Thankful who could run and swim in a rag of a bathing suit and mind no one, dragged her dress over her head with her very skin turning to goose flesh.

"Sort of skinny, ain't she?" observed Ethel with relish.

"You do it with exercise," Mary Curtis comforted her stout daughter-in-law.

Thankful shot a delighted glance at her mother. It might not be so bad with her on your side. She reached for the stiff pink cube which Ethel handed her and stopped smiling. "Put the girdle on first," Ethel commanded briskly.

Thankful passed it back. "I'll need none," she said.

Ethel referred the matter at once to authority. "If she's going to wear the clothes we went to great pains to get her, Mother Curtis," she pronounced, "she'll have to wear 'em over something besides her skin."

Mary Curtis looked doubtful. "Losh!" she muttered. "Well, pull it on you."

Thankful pulled it on. Her mother had failed her, too. She felt as if an iron clamp was gripped about her waist. Did people who wore girdles always have to stand up? You couldn't sit down. Oh, well, she knew what she *could* do. And she waited secure in that knowledge.

The underwear was not bad, there was so little of it. And stockings, if she must wear them, might better be this sleazy kind. But the dresses! One after another Thankful pulled them on and off, and knew without exactly knowing what had happened, that she had lost all color and grace.

"Makes her look sort of washed out," commented Gladys over a red and black plaid. "But she needs a little rouge. I'll show her how to put it on. This is really very smart. The newest thing for young girls."

Thankful felt sick. Her mother looked at her, pale and tall, but trembling a little like a young birch. "Enough's enough," she pronounced. "It's wearfu' business. We like

62

them fine, and if you come down to the kitchen I'll settle for them with you."

They left the room regretfully. Thankful listened until their voices sounded at the foot of the stairs. Then she stripped off the trumpery down to her slim body, the tender skin marked with red lines from its pressure. In a minute she was in her old gingham, out the front door, and down to the dinghy where Limpy had returned for an impatient snooze. She rowed sharply out through the water golden with late light, and hoisted her sails.

As the boat slipped out into deep water, well away from the island, she lifted a long hard cube from the seat and dropped it overboard. She watched it sink, pink and stiff to the last glimpse, down, down; she doubled far over the edge as the boat swung over it. "Let a mermaid try wearing a girdle awhile," she said. With a great sigh she straightened and felt her body grow light and supple again.

Mary Curtis never asked about the girdle. When Thankful got home after a quick sail through the amber twilight of the fall, the house was empty and quiet. Her room was orderly with its own homely things as usual. A quick look in the closet showed her that the new clothes had taken themselves away, temporarily at least. She shuddered at the memory of them. Downstairs her father smoked his pipe in the kitchen while her mother set out the cold chicken and bread and butter for Sunday night supper. "Bring the milk from the well-house," Mary Curtis said.

Even in the short time that she had been indoors, the darkness had fallen. The bright amber had all gone out of the west except one clear line. It looks like a new moon sky, she thought, and turned to see the thin thread curving the sky. She bent her head back, back, to the star-studded arch above her. Where could she ever see sky from earth-edge to earth-edge except on her island? Her throat ached and the stars blurred. She reached into the blackness of the well-house and felt around in the damp for the milk pail.

Migrating Time

The frosts came early that September, hurrying everybody into activity. The stinging smell of piccalilli and chili sauce was pungent through the house as Mary Curtis filled her jars for the winter. The fruits were already in labeled rows in the cellar. The vegetables as they had ripened, peas, beans, greens, were added to the shelves for the long months when the island must be self-contained.

Even jars of young chicken stood ready for the days when the fowl must be kept for eggs and meat was hard to get. Mary Curtis saw to it that her family was well fed during the cold winters, though she found it hard nowadays to cut her provisions to the needs of so few of them. Always the spring saw rows of jars still full of good food. And then the daughters-in-law had a way of drifting into the cellar and admiring its provisions knowing well that a basket of the jars would go back in the motorboat with them. After all, Mary Curtis thought, it was the boys' appetites which had got her into the habit of oversupply and they might as well eat what was meant for them.

Thankful liked best the apple picking. The orchard was so old that even Gramp had not been sure who planted it. But perhaps because it had been kept clean of main-land pests by the wide bay, or because each owner had trimmed and cared for it, it still flowered into fragrant blossoms each spring and ripened into fragrant fruit each fall. Thankful hardly knew when she liked it most.

The Hubbardstons were ready for picking and by the look of the sky, a wind might take them off by tomor-row. They were Thankful's favorite apple and her father had promised her a box to take to school if she would gather them. She picked one and bit into it, cold, juicy, and wondered how it would taste in a strange room shut away from this blue windy sky. She began to pick, hard, fast, that she might not know.

In the alders beyond the orchard a young peabody bird tried his notes, quavered, stopped, tried again a faint sweet whistle. Thankful stopped to listen, and thought it was the loneliest sound of the fall. It felt its way so patiently, so touchingly, toward the full-throated whistle of spring. And when she thought of spring, the road to it seemed lonelier than the whitethroat's whistle. Again she fell to picking the apples.

The barrel was nearly full when she heard the putt-putt of her father's boat returning. She followed idly the sounds of the mooring with the splash of the oars as he came ashore. But she did not turn until she heard steps coming over the grass toward her.

"Why, Dave, where'd you come from?" she cried. "You couldn't have said a word all the way in! I was listening."

"Your Pa's no talker." Dave lifted an apple from the top of the barrel, and Thankful took it away from him. "All right, I'll pick my own." He bit into one which hung high, even with his head. Thankful laughed. They went on picking together as if they had never stopped.

"Going to stay over Sunday?" Thankful asked comfortably.

"Mmm." Dave left the apple so that he could talk. "Had a stroke of luck. Met your Pa just as I was taking some boxes down to the dock for him. For you, I mean."

"Me? What was in 'em?"

"Didn't open 'em. But Gladys mentioned they were hats."

67

"Hats!" Thankful scowled under her brows at Dave and he fended off her look with his spread hand. "What do I want of hats?"

"I wouldn't know about that." Dave peered at her behind his hand. "But she seemed to."

"She would," growled Thankful.

"Come on," said Dave reasonably, "you don't have to wear them picking apples. I'm not Gladys. Don't try to scare me with that look."

Thankful laughed reluctantly. "I'm not. I'd know better."

They picked again in companionable silence.

"Haven't seen you since you ditched the girls. They told me!" Dave grinned reminiscently. "Makes it swell for you, but how you think a feller is ever going to see you again?"

"Well, I don't know. You'll be going off yourself if . . ."

"Know what I came over to tell you?" Dave interrupted.

Thankful looked up into his expectant eyes. "Dave, you didn't! The exams! You didn't really—pass them?"

"Every blamed one." Dave tried to conceal his pride and gave it up. "And that's not all either."

"The job?" Thankful was breathless at the speed that things were going. "Did you get an appointment so soon?"

Dave nodded. "On our own government cutter! Can you beat that?"

Thankful couldn't. She forgot all her own plans and worries in her honest pleasure. They talked about it until the second barrel was filled and the air grew frosty with approaching evening. Then with a basket of the most flawless apples for her school box, they walked toward the house with it swinging between them. The island was very still. No cricket had ever come across to break its silence. No bird sang now.

Suddenly Thankful stopped. "We're growing up," she said desperately. "You are like a man now—and I must go away from the island—and—and"—her voice broke—"even Limpy is growing wild and strong. He's away every day—oh, Dave—oh, Dave . . ."

She could not have borne it if Dave had laughed at her. Though it all sounded so foolish. But he was very tender with a big arm around her shoulders and a grimy hand-kerchief for her tears. She leaned against him comforted. And never lifted her eyes to see the way he was looking down on her fair head against his sleeve.

"Dave," she said solemnly, "I ought to be entering the school for feeble-minded in Augusta. Don't mind me."

Dave drew away from her. "That's not so easy," he said.

Thankful moved on, vaguely uncomfortable. She felt for the old footing and found it. "We're going to have clam fritters for supper. I dug the clams."

Dave looked worried. "You didn't know I was coming.

Do you think you dug enough?" But they both knew that Mary Curtis never had too little of anything.

Thankful ignored the three square boxes on her bed, but after supper Mary Curtis sent for them. "Now we'll try on the hats," she said. Dave brought the boxes down to the kitchen and she took the hats one by one out of the tissue wrappings. Thankful crouched by the fire, glowering at them. "Which one," she asked Dave, "do you think is the worst?"

Dave couldn't tell. "The girls like color, don't they?" he said.

The hard red saucer that was obviously meant to be worn with the red and black plaid Thankful took from her mother and started toward the fireplace. Her father's gruff "Hey!" stopped her. It was of course his money. She put the hat down distastefully. Burned or not, I'll never wear it, she thought. Under the bright blue felt her hair flew out like a dandelion top. And the green one shut down over her like a diver's bell. To face a new school with one of those things on her head was to Thankful unthinkable. Dave looked puzzled at her transformation, and concerned. Her mother was brisk and interested. "It's the way they wear them," she said. "No use fashing yourself." She packed them away in their boxes again. Out of the gloomy silence Thankful stalked off to bed. Dave stared thoughtfully after her.

The next morning he had finished his breakfast when

Thankful came down for her swim. He turned up his collar and shivered. "Every morning until I go," Thankful announced.

"They'll have tubs there, crazy." Dave shuddered down into his coat. "And nice hot water," he shouted after her as she raced down to the icy bay.

When she came down to breakfast Dave looked pleased with himself. "If you hustle," he said, "you can go out with me to pull the lobster pots."

"On Sunday!" she gasped at her father who looked uncomfortable.

"Shut up!" muttered Dave. "Sure, it's necessary work today. The pots need attention what with this wind and your father off yesterday. I'll see you down there," and he started for the shore before Jonathan Curtis could change his mind about breaking the Sabbath.

Thankful ran no risks either after her first shocked exclamation. She buttered two hot muffins, then after a moment's thought, a third one, and raced down to the dinghy which Dave had just finished emptying. As she expected he took one of the muffins which he put in his pocket while he rowed out to the powerboat. Thankful pulled her overalls out of the sailboat as they passed it, and they were all set.

"A shame to waste this breeze on an engine!" Thankful munched the muffins. "Dave, you don't need that muffin in your pocket. You had a good breakfast."

Dave took it out and ate it. Thankful sighed.

Outside the bay was feather white. Dave was in his element. He headed the boat straight up to each marker and when Thankful pulled up the spray hood, threw it back with a clash. The gleaming water poured off their yellow slickers, the green lobsters writhed on the slippery deck, the slatted pots rose from dark depths, emptied, and fell again. The boy and girl laughed and pulled at the slimy ropes until every last pot had been rebaited. Then they scudded home before the wind and under a sky filled now with high clouds. They grew quiet under the heave and fall of the boat rushed forward by each wave. I'm being carried along before the wind, too, Thankful thought, and I can't stop myself.

Jonathan Curtis was better satisfied with the size of the haul than the need of making it on the Sabbath. "I'll give you a run over to the mainland myself," he even offered after dinner when he saw his wife packing up what was left of the apple pie for Dave.

Thankful looked at the dishes stacked in the sink. "I'd just as soon," she said. "I'd rather."

Dave grinned at Mary Curtis. "Would you?" he asked.

"I'd like it fine." She handed the package to Dave. "She's a better sailor than dishwasher."

"We sail." Thankful was firm. "I'm sick of engines."

Enough of the wind had gone down with the tide to

leave a steady breeze. The boat heeled down on her side with a fair wind straight for the mainland dock. Thankful slouched under the tiller, and then got up regretfully. "You can take her over, I suppose, if I bring her back."

Dave took her place. "Now, no advice," he said, "I can run this boat as well as you can."

They slashed along under the silent drive of the wind. Halfway across a great gull swooped around the boat and then dropped gently to the bowsprit. Thankful nodded at Dave. "You see, he can fly as well as I can." Limpy ignored her, dipping pleasantly with the rise and fall of the keel.

The dock lay ahead of them, curiously idle and empty except for a Sunday afternoon pair sitting on a pile of rope. "Glad I'm most through there," said Dave. "First of the week I get my papers. Of course it's slow season on the boat from now on, but it's a good time to learn the ropes."

Thankful sighed. "I wish I wanted to get away as much as you do, Dave."

Dave stared thoughtfully at the pair on the wharf. The man had his arm around the girl. Then he looked at Thankful hauling in the jib. "You know what we might do, Thankful," he called out to her. "Come over here a minute, can't you?"

"Just a jiff." She made the sail fast. "What do you want?"

"I got an idea." Dave looked quite excited. "Now you

don't want to go off to school, and I got a good job."

Thankful perched on the centerboard and stared at him. "Well, what of it?"

Dave's sunburn seemed to deepen. "Why, you hang around the island another year or so—you know, doing things you want to—and I'll get promoted—and then"—he waved an explanatory hand at the couple now near enough to look embarrassed—"why then, we could hitch up, too." He brought the boat up into the wind and held her there fluttering while he waited for Thankful's decision.

Thankful continued to stare at him, but as if she did not really see him. "Well, now that's good of you, Dave, to think of that," she finally said. "But you know a funny thing happened when you said hang round the island a year or two. *I didn't want to!* I've thought such a lot about how awful it would be to go that I guess I kind of want to try it." She looked amazed.

Dave gave the sail a whiff of wind and slid her expertly up to the wharf. "Oh, well," he said, "might as well try it. You and I and the gull." They watched Limpy float his great wings over the dock with an expectant eye for dead herring. "But it wasn't a bad idea at all. It might work out yet." He brought his eyes back to Thankful's startled face. "Well, good-bye. I won't be seeing you again with us both leaving so soon." He kissed her gently and leaped up on the wharf. From there he grinned down at her.

"I'll be sending a good-bye present over by your Pa," he announced, "and I bet you'll like it."

Thankful shoved the tiller over and crawled out into the wind. What would Dave think of next! What utter crazy nonsense! She waved an old paint rag at him and headed up for the island. He was good to try to save her from going off to school. Her heart warmed. He always did stand by me. Limpy flew swiftly after the *Gramp* and caught at his perch. Thankful reached under the seat and pulled out the pie box. As long as he forgot it, she thought, we might as well eat it. She divided it with the gull who swallowed his share whole and watched hers with small greedy eyes.

Then she felt better. But she couldn't get over her astonishment that down somewhere in a depth that she had not probed, she really wanted to try herself out. And with that knowledge the gloom which had darkened her spirit for so long lifted like fog and let in the light. She sprang to her feet and steering the boat with the slight pressure of her body against the tiller, she sang. When had she done this before? Let them try to catch her! Let them try to catch her! Just a twinge, and the recollection was gone.

The island was good, but so might be the rest of the world. And she could come back to it. Maybe sometime with Dave. But that was all as vague as her promise to Gramp about marrying the sea captain and settling down.

Now she was young and strong and filled with zest. The sun dropped, the sky darkened behind the stars, and the sea under them, the wind touched the tops of the sails just enough to drift her into the mooring. The gull's impatient wings took him out of her sight. But when she ran up the path toward the yellow squares of the lighted windows, the homesick pain at leaving them was gone.

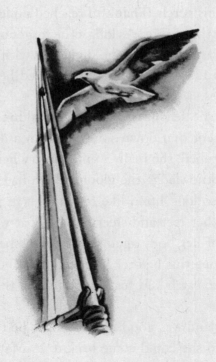

PART II

Away from Bright Island

A Strange Land About Her

Not really gone, she found, when the day came for sailing away from Bright Island. And she thought as she looked back at the silver-gray house softly touched by the silver-gray fog that the homesick pain would always be as much a part of her as her knowledge of every turn of the roof, every pane of the windows which watched her until she lost them in the mist. That other day when she had thought herself free from the place must have come from some odd excitement stirred by Dave's words. If he had asked her this morning, she would stay, she would do anything to deliver herself from this ache in her throat, in her heart. But Dave was on the deck of his cutter, and she was here in the motorboat with her little haircloth trunk beside her well covered with her old slicker to keep it dry.

"Pa, could I take the wheel?" If she could get her hands at work maybe her heart would hurt less.

"I don't know as I would." If Jonathan Curtis was moved by the departure of his last child from the island where he had expected them all to settle comfortably around him in houses of their own, he meant to reveal no softening. Mary Curtis had cried a little down there on the beach when they rowed away from her in the dinghy. Though Thankful knew well enough that she was even now deep in the vegetable cellar sorting the winter turnips. Her mother knew, Thankful realized suddenly, how to turn her feelings into doing things. She'd try again.

"Why not, Pa?" Her throat would hardly let her talk. "I'll watch the compass. And anyway the fog is glinting."

He shook his head without looking at her. "No handling a boat in those clothes, my girl."

She agreed with him bitterly. The slippery new soles and high heels of her shoes were never meant to stand on. The tight-sleeved coat could never swing the arc of the tiller. She crouched beside her trunk and stared out through the fog at the gull wings which cut into it and out. One of those free wild birds might be hers, she thought, though now he was hers no more than Bright Island, and the silver-gray house, and the small sailboat hauled above high water and covered with canvas for the winter. She felt suspended in space between the things which had anchored her and had now let her go, and the unknown anchorage which the future might give her. It was an odd floating feeling which made her giddy and lost. She wished that she could grasp the hard smooth wheel with her two hands. But then she saw her fingers stiffened in their new gloves and felt as if they would never bend around good hard wood again.

The boat pushed on down the shore, never even coming in sight of the wharf where she had so often dropped Dave. Down the coast to the big harbor where Thankful had never been. Nor indeed had Jonathan gone there often, and his whole mind was set on the channel buoys appearing and disappearing in shadowy warning. He was going at low speed now and he passed the horn to Thankful. All around them the fog had come alive with nervous hoots held into constant rhythm by the unexcited who-o-o-o of the foghorn at the lighthouse. It steadied Thankful and she slipped her horn's beat into it, one, two, three.

Then they were at the dock where men rushed about instead of leaning idly against the piles to watch you land. Thankful looked at her father when he had made the boat fast, and knew that he had no more idea than she had about what to do next. She could feel him hating to leave his boat. She pulled off the old rain cape and folded it on the seat. From a box under it she took out Dave's present which had come over by boat only the day before. She had only to look at it to feel again that warm gratitude that made Dave suddenly near and dear. He had saved her from the horror of the red and black hat with this small neat casque which fitted closely over her fair hair. It was not even uncomfortable! How could Dave have known so exactly what to get! She could see him, big and clumsy in the shop, fingering the hopeless muddle which she would never have faced, and finally balancing this small blue felt on the tip of one great finger for the saleswoman to wrap. Her eyes stung as she smoothed it and turned to Jonathan stowing away and tying down everything removable on his boat.

"The bus is where they said it would be, Pa," she told him. "If you'll take the trunk over there to it, you won't need to get out of sight of the boat. I can manage the rest of the way."

Jonathan looked up from the compass which he was locking into the diddy box. Thankful knew his relief, and how he would feel when he could set up that compass and go sailing away from this noisy harbor. She knew how he would feel. And she must go on the other way. For one hot, wild flash her spirit flung itself back with him,

82

and she was chugging home to the peace of the warm kitchen, and her wide-open windows under the eaves. She was amazed to find herself climbing the slippery dock ladder and leaning over to help Jonathan swing the trunk up from the dinghy. You went right on, she decided, after you had once started because part of you had to stay steady even when all the rest was shaken. She walked over to the bus which stood empty except for the driver who hoisted the small trunk to the top with a swing of one arm.

Jonathan stood awkwardly at the window where he could watch his boat. "Good-bye," he said, and she thought that he bent forward to kiss her, but the bus shot ahead with a whoosh, and Thankful saw him lope back to the edge of the dock.

She suddenly knew great relief, as if some hard struggle had come to an inevitable conclusion. She need fight herself no more about going ahead. She was cut away from the last mooring. She had no choice but to go on. The youth rose in her and tugged her on, as it had away from Dave when he had asked her to stay. She settled back against the cushions and pondered with great interest on the ugliness of the passing town.

The bus turned into a wide street so crowded with trolley cars and automobiles that Thankful could not believe it would find space for itself. The rush of the cars past the window made her draw her head in and edge out on the seat. The clang and roar beat like heavy surf over her, yet there was something oddly exciting about the way she was dashed through it. She held her breath as if she were about to swim under water.

The driver slewed around a corner and ducked his head in at Thankful at the same instant. Her breath whistled through her teeth, but miraculously she was still afloat. "Got to meet a train," he announced and pulled in to the curb just as a great engine roared into the station. The noise of the street was but a faint murmur behind it. She clapped her hands over her ears and even her hands were strange in their stiff gloves. She reassured herself with a swift recollection of the picture of the school, quiet and high on a hill.

She dropped her hands in her lap tight closed together. The driver was not bringing freight, but girls and boys, the street suddenly alive with them. Behind them poured porters with neat strapped bags and coats and pigskin cases spattered with odd bright labels. Great trunks filled the platform by the baggage car. The driver flung a handful of checks at a truckman and hoisted the bags up beside her trunk. Instantly the bus was full of young people. Thankful had never seen so many together in her life. Nor could she think of any live creatures, wild cattle ranging in pasture, porpoises slashing under her boat, she could think of none so terrifying as this milling bright group full of laughter.

From her corner her eyes followed them warily until

she realized that they saw her no more than the spare tire. Once a tall dark boy swayed with the bus against her. He smiled down at her with a brief, "Sorry," and returned to the girl beside him, her arm locked in his for steadiness. The two seemed to know each other well, she thought. Her intent eyes dodged through the crowded bus to see them. They called to each other and their speech sounded odd to Thankful and pushed her still further outside like a foreigner. Nothing on the island had prepared her for these bright creatures!

She remembered how Gladys had scorned them as stuck-up, and thought how easy it would be if she, Thankful, were now sitting at a high school desk with her own kind of people around her. But she still wanted stubbornly not to be there. The island would not bear thinking about, but living with Gladys was another matter.

The bus, well out of town now, swept along a shore road with gray waves swishing against it. Thankful was glad that the fog was too thick for her to see the outlying islands. Her lungs caught at the salt damp air as if they had stopped breathing through the city. The boy in front of her bent down to the open window where his face was on a level with hers. "Smells good, doesn't it?" he said, and she nodded breathlessly. He straightened up and Thankful knew that he hadn't even seen her.

Some sensitive plate in her mind had registered his face, clear and dark, and she thought how unlike Dave and her brothers he was. He seemed so carefully made, as finished as a beautiful sloop. Even his voice was different, clipped and sure. When he said, "Chicago doesn't smell like that!" Thankful thought how far to come to school, and her own island seemed suddenly near.

"Clam flats!" sniffed the girl who clung to his arm. And Thankful laughed because the tide was in.

The boy bent again, his eyes searching the cove. "If Donnel hasn't put my boat off . . ." He frowned into the fog—then, "It's there! It's there!" and Thankful for the life of her could not help turning her head to see it.

He had a boat, that boy, a beautiful expensive-looking knockabout, polished and fine like himself. Swifter than the *Gramp*, she conceded, but not so staunch. I could out-sail him in a stiff breeze, she thought, and then remembered that there was no chance. It was as if a candle had been lighted and then blown out. Then it was Robert this, and Robert that, as if they all liked him and his boat.

The bus left the sea so suddenly that Thankful had not known it was gone until she felt thick smooth air in nostrils which knew only the sharp tang of the ocean. Her head went up, alarmed like a deer, at the close pressure of the trees over the bus. The car moved swiftly through the shut-in road, straight inland. Even the mainland had never had this close heavy smell! It must be better, she thought, when she could get out of the bus. Six miles from the sea, the catalogue had said. And already she felt as if she were a fish gasping for the wash of the cold water across its gills.

Mile after mile. Then the bus swerved through stone posts up a gravel drive and gritted to a stop before the white colonial house of the catalogue. Thankful's ears hummed and she felt as if she were still rushing on though she sat immovable in her corner. She watched the bright stream of boys and girls pour out between the pillars and knew that she must follow them.

Thankful sat there. What was she doing here? Daughter of an islander, thrust into a life which had nothing to do with her. Which never could take her in. She would go back. But what of Gramp, she suddenly thought. Daughter of an islander, but granddaughter of a sea captain who sailed himself into every port. She walked out of the bus through the wide door of the great house.

She went through the office where she signed her name and answered the questions of a worried little man, and then back into the hall to claim her luggage with the rest. They were clustered about her small trunk, and the girl whom Robert had called Selina was bending over it in laughter. Thankful saw how strange it looked among the thick-skinned bags and she hardly knew how to claim it. She stood quietly waiting until Selina straightened up and saw her.

"Oh, it's yours." The girl continued to smile. "Isn't it cute? I'll tell John to take it around with the other maids' luggage."

Thankful knew nothing to say except the truth. "I'm not a maid. I am going to study here."

The rest of the crowd had backed away and she could hear the high chatter of their voices drifting until they no longer pressed upon her. She gained confidence. "Yes," she repeated, "I'm going to study here. And this is my trunk." She looked at the slip in her hand. "It is to go to room 312."

"My Lord!" The girl stared at her with round blue eyes. "Look what I've drawn!" And she held out a slip marked 312.

Thankful shook her head. "I don't know what you mean. Is there a mistake that we both have the same number?" She was finding it hard to breathe.

"It means—oh, my Lord!—it means . . ." The tragic intensity made Thankful tremble. "It means that we are roommates!"

It had not occurred to Thankful that she might be put in the room with someone else. She had always had her own room. And to be penned up with this girl who looked upon her as a servant! "I don't like this any better than you do," she said surprisingly. "Come back in the office where we got the numbers."

A tall woman had come into the room while they had been gone and Thankful recognized the look of her own people in her. "Don't go near her," Selina whispered, "she's as hard as nails. Wait until Dinsie comes back. I can manage him."

Thankful paid no heed. "We can't have this arrange-ment." She presented the slips to the woman. "Please give me a room to myself."

Selina began to chatter beside her. "Probably some mistake . . . You remember . . . How well you look, Miss Haynes . . . My mother sent her love."

Miss Haynes looked gravely at Thankful. "Who are you?" she asked. "And why do you want a change?"

Thankful's steady eyes met hers under dark brows. "I am the granddaughter of Captain Curtis," she said, "and I come from Bright Island."

Miss Haynes nodded. "I know. Never been away before?"

Thankful felt a queer choke in her throat. "No. May I please have a room to myself? Any little one?" She had a sudden thought. "Perhaps a maid's room?" She was grate-ful to Selina for the idea.

Miss Haynes continued to look at her thoughtfully. "Your grandfather thought that you would feel this way about rooming alone," she said. "He talked with me about it when he came down to look the school over. He didn't expect you would come so soon, you see."

Thankful's eyes stung with the seeing. Gramp had been down there getting things ready for her! And he hadn't known that he was going to leave her there so soon.

Selina's voice jerked her back. It sounded as if she were trying to cover the eagerness with sweet words. "Evelyn

Norris and I are rooming together this year. You remember, Miss Haynes. You were so nice about helping us settle it. We have it all planned. . . ."

"Yes, yes." Miss Haynes was suddenly impatient. "But Evelyn has unexpectedly gone to Europe with her mother for a few months. Perhaps at the Christmas holidays we can make a change. Now it must stand. This application came in so late that Evelyn's was the only vacant place." She brushed past them and left them staring at each other.

Selina's prettiness was washed over by a red tide of fury. "And I must room with you!" she said.

Thankful glowered at her under dark brows. "And I must room with you!" she said.

Selina stepped back, startled.

"Hi, Selina." The boy, Robert, peered into the room. "Well, you're a friendly-looking pair. What's up?"

Selina changed under their eyes and, while Thankful still stormed, laughed airily up at the boy. "Allow me to present you to my new roommate," she said, but her voice cracked a little.

Robert whistled softly and started to speak but Selina seized his arm and pulled him toward the door. He turned and caught Thankful's desolate look which followed them. "Oh, cheer up," he said, "Selina's a good egg." And for all his light words his smile was understanding. It touched Thankful's sore spirit.

Thankful wandered out into the hall with her 312

ticket pinched in her fingers. What now? The hail chattered like a blackbird roost. Miss Haynes, like a larger blackbird, detached herself and swooped down on Thankful. "This way," she said.

They climbed a broad curved staircase and turned down a long corridor where through open doors girls were calling excitedly to each other. Thankful had never seen so large a house. At the end of the hall Miss Haynes opened a door with 312 on it in small brass numbers. "Your trunk will be up soon," she said. "Dinner at seven." She gave Thankful a worried busy smile and hurried away.

Thankful leaned against the closed door and looked around the room. The early fall twilight had darkened the corners and pressed against the shut windows. The room smelled clean and unused. Even Thankful's unaccustomed eye knew that it was right in its cool green and white. But two beds, two chests of drawers, two mirrors, two, two, two, never herself by herself again. The shabby room under the eaves crept through these wide walls, and Thankful had to shut her eyes to send it away.

When she opened them the dark seemed nearer and she pushed a window wide to feel it, intimate and close like the island twilight. But it beat against her with that odd thick smell of land air. Leaves, she thought, getting ready to fall, and weeds and earth. We have them all on the island but the air from the sea washes them clean. It seemed somehow as if life suddenly pressed around her, in the same way, thick and dark and foreign. In a panic she leaned far out of the window for something tangible and real.

Squares of golden light spaced evenly the shadowy stone house across the campus. Thankful could hear the boys' voices, deeper but as excited as the girls'. She tried to think how it would feel to be so glad to see people, and gave it up. Probably Robert lived over there and he was telling them about Chicago, and what a wonderful boat he had, and—oh, her own little boat! If it were only free under the stars with the gull riding in the prow . . .

She drew her head in and found the room quite dark. Selina must be in soon. Where was the lamp? But of course there were no lamps here filled with kerosene to be lighted with a match. What did you do to make an electric light burn? She couldn't bear to have Selina find her sitting there in the dark.

A bang at the door. "Trunk, Miss!" It wasn't Selina yet.

"Oh, yes. And please turn on my light." The room flared into whiteness, and Thankful's little trunk was sitting in the corner. As strange out of its garret as she was!

She walked over to the wall and examined some knobs. The boy had punched something here, she decided, and pushed a button. The light did not flicker. She pushed another, and the room was black. A knock sounded so close to her ear that she jumped. Selina, perhaps! In a panic she pushed both buttons.

"I'm here," said a plaintive voice, "you don't have to

ring again," and a neat little maid walked into the room.

Thankful looked at her. Now how in the world had she got her? Anyway the light was on.

"Did you want something?" the girl was asking, and Thankful heard the speech of her own coast, quick and light.

Thankful thought hard. What could she ask for? "Water?" she suggested.

"I'll show you the bathroom," the girl said primly.

Thankful blinked at the glitter of tiles, the white porcelain under the glare of the ceiling light. "How did you turn it on?" she pointed overhead. This was a point to be checked on before Selina arrived.

The girl laughed but her contempt did not sound ill-natured. "You must be a hick!" She pressed the button on and off. "My goodness, we've had electric lights for ages at Ledgtown where I live."

"I am from Bright Island," said Thankful proudly.

"Oh." The girl looked at her with round eyes. "You a Curtis?"

Thankful nodded.

"Well! That's why you got such a good room. That Selina White knows everybody. And she's got scads of money. You'll have a swell time!" She backed toward the stairs. "My name's Edie. Better get dressed for dinner," she advised.

Thankful was puzzling over the lettered faucets.

When H was tempered with C, she splashed her face and hands. I'll try that tub tonight, she thought. I hope there'll be enough hot water to fill it. Now what did Edie mean about getting dressed for dinner? This is my best dress. She looked down distastefully at the red and black plaid.

Back in her room every chair and one of the beds was piled high with clothes. Selina, bare armed, distracted, pulled at the masses of soft colors, discarding this one, frowning at that. A wardrobe trunk gaped and another, big and important, spilled its contents on the rug. The room suddenly felt very full.

Thankful watched the upsetting process a moment. "Lost something?" she inquired.

Selina made no answer but dove into a wisp which Thankful supposed might be a dress. "Here, fasten this, will you? What was that funny name Miss Haynes called you?"

"I didn't hear her call me anything funny," Thankful told her without moving to touch the dress.

"Your name! That funny name! And for goodness' sake help me!" Selina whirled impatiently toward her.

"My name is Thankful Curtis"—even to Selina the words took on dignity and beauty—"and remember I explained once about not being one of the maids."

Selina stared at her and fumbled at her own hooks.

Thankful reached for them. "I'd be glad to help you." How smooth and white and soft the girl was! And what kind of a party could she be going to in this lovely thing? Thankful scarcely dared touch it with her brown outdoor fingers.

"All right." Selina became gracious as she looked at herself in the mirror. "You don't really need to dress for dinner this first night. Lots of the trunks haven't come."

So this was what dressing for dinner meant! Thankful looked down at her red and black plaid. Well, she thought, they might just as well get used to seeing me this way. They can't hate it any worse than I do.

A mellow gong sounded downstairs. Selina fled. "When you're ready," she flung back, "go down to the hall. Miss Haynes will give you a seat at the table."

Thankful stared at the closed door. What had Miss Haynes told her? That they all sat where they pleased the first night. Well, it hadn't pleased Selina to sit with her. Wouldn't it be better to go to bed without any dinner than to face that crowd alone? Thankful considered. She had never felt so queer inside and she didn't know whether she was ill or very hollow. It had been a long fast. She decided to break it. After all, she thought, they didn't even see me in the bus and they'll have something else to look at now. There'll be Selina, for one thing. She made herself open the door and go down the long staircase. She moved as if she were walking in her sleep.

The rest was the confusion of sleep, blurred, unreal. Through a haze she saw a great golden room filled with high lights, and color, and still the same laughter. Though she was not of it, she sat there in it. The girls cast swift glances under their lids at her clothes and talked on to the boys. The boys did not see her at all. An occasional older person, perhaps a teacher, spoke to her. She had thought she could not eat with the terror of it, and then a maid slipped a small scooped dish past her, and she caught the rich buttery odor of clam chowder. And the kitchen at home! Her mother stood by the stove ladling it out into big white bowls with crisp chowder crackers. For a moment the odds were even for homesickness and hunger. She did not know which would win when she lifted the spoon automatically. Then with the taste of the hot chowder the tightness of her throat relaxed so that she could swallow again.

"Swell to get seafood again, isn't it?" someone spoke beside her, and she answered yes, yes it was. And wished for the deep white bowl at home. Though she forgot that wish soon. The other girls touched their food lightly and left it, as they sighed over the pounds gained last term. Thankful looked at her empty plate and thought, I might have gone to bed and missed this!

Then her lids felt heavy on her eyes, and the bright room swam in her sleepiness. She pushed against the deadweight on her senses to make her ears listen to what seemed to be a speech of welcome from a pleasant dry-looking man. She rose with the rest but she stumbled a little. This numb fatigue bore no relation to the way she felt after a day of haying or digging clams. No one saw her drift away from the tide of young people in the hall. She thought that she knew how a shadow felt.

The bath was astonishing. A stream of water without end, and no pumping or heating. It stretched her out and eased her aching muscles. Though why, she thought, my legs should ache when I've not had a chance to use them all day, I can't see. She dropped into the cool bed without turning on the light, and slept profoundly.

A glare of light struck her across her eyes and brought her up with a confused sense that it was lightning and that her mother wanted her to shut the windows before the storm broke. She sat up while sleep drifted away like a fog and let her see through it. This was not home, and that girl tossing things from her bed was Selina with whom she must share her life. She wished that it had been lightning, and that it had struck her. She lay down again and tried to close her eyes against the white glare overhead.

When Selina banged out to the bathroom, Thankful rose and pressed the button which she hoped was the right one. Selina muttered angrily when she stumbled back into the dark room, but she turned on the soft bedside light. She closed all of the windows except the one over Thankful's bed which she could not reach. Then after some odd and elaborate preparation of her hair, she turned out the light and Thankful knew by her deep breathing that she slept almost at once.

Again the dark pressed around Thankful, thick and foreign. She sat up and tried to get the air from her window but it seemed so small an amount that it wasn't worth struggling for. Not a light on the campus. But no quiet. The screech, screech, screeching of the crickets she recognized from her mainland experience, but that quick angry scrape which beat regularly through their rasp was a file on her tired nerves. "It's probably katydids," she told herself, remembering how she had always wanted to hear them. "I wish they'd stop!"

Her first deep sleep broken, that path of escape was closed. She must lie in this airless black space with only the realization of how inevitably it must go on—and on— and on. Its very limitless expanse dazed her imagination into sleep again. The first day was over.

Learning that Lies in Books

Thankful listened and watched. With people all around her she could not think. Easy enough at the old kitchen table with her mother moving quietly about, now and then bending over her, a spicy cake pan in her hand, or sitting in the rocker while Thankful chanted her Latin at her. Easy enough to see what the words and the figures meant then.

She felt that she might have learned to think along with a room full of people if they had all been together, after the same thing. But she was aware of the little clashing thoughts all around her, girls about boys, boys about girls, clothes, hair waves, chances to fool the teacher, all the little ideas running about and into each other. Endless noise and confusion, though the room was quiet. She sat dumb, and listened and watched.

At last she saw that the time would come when she must take her turn at marshalling her thoughts into speech for them all to hear. She was frozen with terror. At the end of the first week, Dr. Davis, the principal, was to decide the puzzling question of how to rank her, this girl who had never been to school. She knew now what he would do. Send her home. And if she could have gone without disgrace, she hoped he might. But to go because she could not do the work—Thankful's pride stung her like a whip.

She had stood, tall and pale when they called on her, and had stood quiet until pityingly they had called on another. Her voice would not come. There was nothing for it to say. Selina made the struggle no easier. "You'll last just about this first week if you don't open your mouth and recite," she told her.

"Well then," agreed Thankful, "you'll have your room to yourself, won't you?"

"Tongue sharp enough sometimes," grumbled Selina.

But Thankful was not aware of sharpness. She was scudding under bare poles now and it needed little more to wreck her. She had no attention for the lesser irritations of Selina. They saw each other seldom except as they saw the furniture of the room. Selina's light quick mind spent little time in work, and Thankful's mind was defending itself against certain doom. She had nothing left in her for the friendly gay encounters which she saw about her. Among the other girls and boys she was still a shadow.

Toward the end of the week she had tried all of the first year classes, and known that she could not go back to them. It was small satisfaction to her that the lessons when she looked at them in her room were so easy that she could hardly remember when she had not known all about them. All knowledge fled with that terrible pressure of human curiosity and conflict.

She had heard Selina's moans about the Latin and the man who taught it. "He hates us all and he's so beautiful! We adore him! And he's using us only so that he can get another degree. You wait till he gets hold of you. That will finish you!"

Thankful was sure that it would, but she only wanted it over with. She sat in Mr. Fletcher's room and waited for him to finish her. Now that the outcome was certain she relaxed into numb indifference. She even had some attention for the personality of the man, and liked it. He showed off a bit, she thought, but she was used to men.

101

And she recognized the reality of his feeling for Cicero. It was like her mother's. No wonder he raged at the way they read it. She wasn't sure but what he enjoyed being savage. He caught her reflective eye and gave her a brusque nod. "Read that next paragraph as if you were a Roman," he snapped. "What's your name?"

"My name is Thankful Curtis," she said and he checked it off while the class giggled faintly.

"All right, go on," he said, and waited intolerantly.

But Thankful had spoken. She had heard her own voice. She had pronounced her own name. She had announced herself, and she was no longer a shadow. She was real, at least for the moment.

She stood and read the words to him, the old familiar words. How many times had her mother said, "Read them as if you were a Roman," and had read them to her until Thankful saw her a Roman matron instead of a Scotch woman kneading bread. She read them as she knew them, unaware of amused glances and lifted eyebrows.

Mr. Fletcher slammed his book and she jumped, startled into silence. Around her all that pressure, all that criticism, and the man at the desk staring at her . . .

"For the love of heaven," he said as if he could not bear it, "where did you go to school?"

The class applauded him with a giggle. He scowled at them.

Thankful reached the end of her endurance.

"Nowhere," she said clearly and she did not care what any of them thought. "I live on an island and my mother taught me." She was indifferent to the wholehearted laughter of the class.

Mr. Fletcher lifted a silencing hand. "The only time that I have heard Latin read like that," he said, "was at Oxford. I wish that you had all been born on islands and taught by your mothers." A gong rang. "Will you wait, Miss Curtis?" and Thankful caught the sudden charm of his smile as the class filed out behind her. Her knees trembled a little.

He talked to her like a human being. Amusingly, as one adult to another. And Thankful, who had known no girls but a whole family of men, felt at home with him at once. Even to telling him how she must go back to the island now. Strangely enough minding the thought of it.

"Utter nonsense," the man said. "Not but what you would be better off with the kind of teaching you've had. But failure's a bad companion to take back with you. Come to my office at four."

The office was a comfortable untidy place. Books scattered over the table as they were in the kitchen. Familiar ones, too. Thankful's experienced eye picked them out. Mr. Fletcher wandered around the room about his own affairs as her mother did. Now and then he talked with her about books she had read. Mostly he smoked his pipe and read.

After a while Dr. Davis sauntered into the room and the two men talked about new bookcases for the library. Thankful paid no attention to them. This was the most peaceful spot that she had found. The tide flowed back over bare and thirsty spaces. She felt refreshed in the vigor of her own thoughts. When Dr. Davis asked her what she was doing she scarcely heard him.

Then it was like a swift game. He moved, and she moved, covering the board on which was written all that she knew. Of course he won, but Thankful had the elation of a good player. Her alert eyes under their dark brows had followed his every move. After her mother had finished a grilling like that, Thankful always leaped for her boat and went singing down the bay. Excitement tingled now like an electric current. Even her fine halo of hair seemed alive with it.

Dr. Davis looked as if he had been having a good time, too. Mr. Fletcher had the air of the cat who had swallowed the canary. He smoked very fast.

"There seems to be a good deal of doubt about George Washington and his successors," Dr. Davis said, and Thankful felt chagrined. "But the Scottish lines are intact."

Thankful ventured that they hadn't done much with the United States yet because it was so new. He said yes, that there was nothing like a good foundation, and wouldn't she like to go out and have a little fun before dinner. Friday afternoons lots of things went on.

Friday afternoon! The time struck her and she staggered. Suddenly she saw the whole thing. They had been giving her the final interview before they sent her home. And she had played it like a game! George Washington! But he had probably only clinched the failures that all the teachers had reported. Go out and have a little fun! The light flowed out of her as if the current had been suddenly turned off.

"I think I'd better do something about getting my father to meet me," she said drearily. "He might be able to come across in his boat Sunday if I could send word tonight."

Mr. Fletcher slammed his pipe down and sprang to his feet. But Dr. Davis laughed at her. "Tut, tut," he said, "we're only settling which classes you'll fit into. Your father won't have to come for you for quite a while. Go on out and have some fun."

They were going to let her stay! She stood outside in the early twilight until she knew that it was so. She looked back at the lights turned on in the study. There she had got glory. Here she would keep it. Shouts across the darkening campus. Other human beings besides herself. She would find out how not to be a shadow. And she would learn about George Washington before she slept—her heart swept forward days ahead.

Saturday morning blew through her window shaking and scattering leaves until she could see patches of sky as blue as island sky. No'west with a bite to it. The bay would be feather white today. She stared up from her bed and saw waves tossing instead of the leaves.

Selina shivered under the covers. "For goodness' sake shut that window. And see if there isn't steam on."

"I'll shut the window." Thankful had wakened to her glory and she would not let it go. "But where do you look for the steam?"

"In the pipes, goose." Selina rose on her elbow. "Turn that wheel."

Thankful knelt like an angel, her hair its halo, to the astonishing rite. And heat was made there in the pipes with odd and guttural sounds. She sat back on her heels and laughed because of her light heart. "The fire is built," she said. "Get up." But Selina went back to sleep again.

Thankful thought about her Saturday and knew what to do with it. Six miles to the sea. She could walk that easily. Would they let her have a lunch? They would. At nine by the chapel clock she went through the gates with her quick light step. But she thought, I can come back through them. I belong.

Halfway to the shore the bus picked her up. Robert had leaned out and called to her. He and his two room-mates of the tower room were off to try his boat.

"Too much wind till the tide turns," said Thankful, weather-wise. But she would have taken out the *Gramp*.

They listened, doubtful. She sounded like one who knew. "Will it go down then?" they asked.

"I should think so." She nodded, not too sure. "Probably get becalmed by afternoon," and she smiled to see them worry.

She left them as soon as the bus turned on the shore. It was not possible to sit in a car on a day like this. If she went up the shore and they went down, she needn't see them again. And Robert's lovely sloop. She skittered along like a sandpiper, her hair blowing in the wind, her feet light on the hard sand. She thought she could never breathe enough of this sharp salt air.

Dark-grained sand, humped rocks sunk in beds of gold wet seaweed, up and up the shore with the tide rushing the feathered waves at her. It hissed into gullies, and sure-footed she leaped them. All about her was the sound of moving water.

When she had gone a long way, she came to a closed rocky cove, shut around like a room. She stripped off her clothes and plunged into the brine and the cold of the sharp waves. She dashed through them as if she breathed water, not air. She floated and watched the waves bear down on her and lift her up. She swam herself into a glow such as she had not felt since she left the island. I could swim back to Bright Island, she thought, and quickly put that thought away.

The sun dried her, the good lunch fed her, and then

she slept, tired with the first real stretch of her muscles. When she woke the sun said mid-afternoon. She must start back. The wind had all gone down as she had prophesied, and the sea lay still and blurry blue. The sharp morning had softened into the fall quiet that Thankful knew on her island.

Just before she had to leave the shore for the road, an old man drove his powerboat up to a rough wharf. She stopped to watch him. He was making a botch of it. She ran down to the end of the landing and caught his painter. "Hurt my wrist hauling," he explained and Thankful knew that he was grumpy because it hurt. She moved handily about the boat making things shipshape. "Pretty good at it, ain't you?" he conceded. "Come from round here?"

"Bright Island," she said and was proud.

"A Curtis, hey? No wonder you can handle a boat." He toiled down the wharf with Thankful at his heels. "What you doing round here?"

Thankful told him.

"Come down next Sat'day and I'll take you out," he grunted.

Thankful could not believe her luck. But he said it again when he saw her face, as if he even understood a little the thirst of her sea-starved soul. "Gorry, you help quite a lot," he said and stumped off across a pasture.

The bus passed her with the boys just as she entered

the gates. They leaned out and waved. It slowed up and she hopped to the steps hanging to the rail as they slithered up the drive. Blown and sunburned and happy!

"Hey, don't fall off there!" That was Robert laughing at her. "Say, we got becalmed all right. Who told you all about the weather?"

"I just know," Thankful called back at him. "It's born in island people."

"Pretty handy," mourned Robert touching gingerly a blister on his palm. "Saves a lot of rowing."

"Where you been all day?" asked one of the boys leaning forward to look at her.

The bus stopped and Thankful leaped off without answering. Robert waved his cap at her and she ran up the steps. She ran as if she had just risen from a night's slumber, and her heart was warm and full.

Five minutes to change from the old blue gingham to an ugly thing from her closet, and she was seated at the table stiff and quiet as ever. Inside though, something had melted and flowed softly through her veins. She had found the sea again, and Robert liked her. Of course it was important, too, that she was to be allowed to stay, but that was old news. Today's sun had poured light into a good many dark corners.

Selina was curious. She had seen the bus drive up and knew who was in it. "Where you been all day?" she asked like the boy.

Thankful answered in the same way. She took her towels and soap and closed the door softly behind her.

When she came back Selina was waiting. "You certainly looked funny hanging onto that bus like a street kid. Lucky no one in the office saw you."

"Did," said Thankful. "Dr. Davis saw me."

"My Heavens! But then I suppose it makes no difference now. When you going?"

"Going where?" Thankful had opened her window, and was stretched in the luxury of the soft bed.

"Home, of course." Selina was sounding crosser.

"Oh, that!" Thankful turned away from the light. "When I'm through here, I guess."

"Well, when's that?" exasperated.

No answer. From the quiet head on the pillow Thankful might be sleeping. Selina knew no way to prove that she wasn't.

Monday morning Thankful was summoned to the office. The old fear rushed back though she tried to still it with what she was sure Dr. Davis had said. He certainly made me think I was going to stay, she thought, but just what did he say? And she could not remember. If I have to go now!

But it proved a business-like encounter which left her rather breathless. She sat at her desk in the study hall and examined the program in her hand. Senior courses all of them except history and German. With a little extra work, he had said, she could finish up this year. Finish up this year! Go back to Bright Island to live! Forever and forever! Her eyes still looked as they had when he made the incredible statement, and followed it with, "Are you then so glad to be through with us?"

"Oh, no!" He must believe that she was not rude. "Not that!" It was no use. She could not explain. She lifted honest distressed eyes to him. "Bright Island is where I belong."

She hoped he understood. He had said, "You'll have to work hard to get back there."

"There's no work too hard for that," she had told him, and he had looked oddly touched.

Suddenly she realized from the blue program in her hand that she should be in a class this moment. Room 212. Senior Latin. She ran for it! Down the long hall! But the door, that implacable door, with seniors behind it, and astonished looks. She fingered the knob. And then somehow she was in, and Mr. Fletcher was glaring at her with his impatient, "Late! Late! What have I—oh, it's you, Miss Curtis. Well, try to be on time after this. Go on, Saunders."

She slid into a seat. There they were, Selina and Robert. She should have known that they would both be in this class. Selina looked horrified, and Robert embarrassed. They think I have made a mistake, thought Thankful, they all do. Maybe I have.

She began to listen to Saunders to find out. He was

pretty bad. Mr. Fletcher's irritation agreed with her. She would have to do better than that. Well, she could. He was good not to call on her until she felt more secure. Perhaps he would skip her this time. Selina had passed a note along to her. "Tell him that you've got in the wrong room." She was honestly distressed. That was nice of Selina. She had made a stumbling translation herself. Perhaps she felt a little responsible if Thankful was to be disgraced before the seniors. The hour was nearly over. Then she heard her name.

"Read the Latin, Miss Curtis, I need not tell you as if you were a Roman."

Thankful caught that sudden charm of his smile, and read.

The class stirred uneasily, ready to laugh, waiting their cue from the master.

"Learn to read your Latin like that," he said benignly and picked up his book.

The class watched him leave the room. They turned a dazed stare on Thankful like one person slowly turning a head. Then they followed him out of the room.

Selina caught her by the arm. "What under the sun!" she whispered angrily. "I tried to save you!"

"Didn't need saving." Thankful felt cool and steady now.

Robert was on the other side now. "Say, that was a grand performance! What do you mean by getting

Fletcher sore at us?" His keen dark face was admiring, interested.

Selina rushed ahead. "Hurry up, Robert. We'll be late to math."

Thankful followed them. She had to go there, too. And math was something you couldn't read out of a book. You had to think about it, alone and quiet.

The room was like a beehive. It quieted when the teacher entered. But the inner noise and confusion went on. Thankful knew that she was finished. Her brain felt like a frozen block. The problems rushed out at the students, and they took them with them to the blackboard. Thankful took hers and stood with it, blank and empty. She heard the rattling of letters and figures around her as the recitations drew nearer her. Then it was her turn. She had not put one figure on the board.

She shook her head, and saw Robert's pitying eyes. The teacher was a stout woman who somehow looked insulted at her refusal. "How do you happen to be in this class?" Her voice said, At least I have a right to know this.

Thankful stood with downcast head. What to say but the truth? "Dr. Davis sent me."

"But why?" This woman was not daunted by Dr. Davis or anybody else. "Why, when you can't understand a simple theorem like this? He has made a mistake."

He had not made a mistake. Thankful lifted her head to catch Selina's triumphant agreement. He had not made a mistake. She would not have him humiliated by her. "I do understand it," she said. "I think I can prove it now."

"Too late. See me after class."

Thankful sat still and waited. She thought someone touched her gently on the shoulder as the class filed out, and she looked up to the dark eyes she was learning to notice. "Sic her!" whispered Robert. "She likes a good fight."

He was gone. And so were the rest. Thankful did not feel like a good fight. She felt like a good run. But Miss Jackson was challenging her through round spectacles. Yet all she said was, "Prove it then." And Thankful proved it. "Stage fright?" she asked. Thankful nodded. "Well, I don't bite." Mary Curtis had been caustic often enough to make Thankful feel at home now. She tried to explain about the business of thinking and Miss Jackson looked interested.

"But you might as well learn to think in a crowd. You can't live like a hermit all your life."

"Yes, I can!" Thankful's face lit with white fire. "I'm going back to Bright Island."

"Not yet, you aren't," the woman said briskly. "You're here to stay for the year, I understand. Now you learn to use the brain God gave you without having to dig yourself into a hole to do it."

"Yes'm," said Thankful meekly, and she thought that she could. After a few more math lessons!

Learning that Lies in People

Thankful now looked about her. She was here to stay irrevocably. You could be alone on an island and not be lonely. She thought how she wandered about day in, day out, berrying, clamming, sailing, and loved her loneliness as freedom. But here that freedom was changed into ostracism by these people milling about her. They worked upon her kind of enjoyment as they did on her thinking. Since she could not go her own ways here, she must learn to go theirs. The Saturdays would still belong to her, and rain or shine, the sea waited for her. But six long days stretched between them, days and evenings filled with activities in which she had no part.

Selina was of little help. She had accepted a sort of academic equality with Thankful because of the increased ease of her own work. Thankful answered questions willingly, and her resources were astounding. Selina grew to rely upon them. Time to her was a thing not to be thrown away on work.

She's as busy as a mink having a good time, Thankful thought wistfully. I seem to have so much time for nothing. Her anxious absorption at the beginning had set her apart, and now she found herself still outside watching all these young people who had no awareness of her. She had thought she could find out how not to be a shadow, but now she was not sure that a shadow could ever become substance.

Each evening when they danced until study hour, Thankful sat in a far corner and watched them. The rhythm beat in her ears and inside she felt herself dancing. Once Robert saw her and said casually, "Dance?" and she shook her head. "I don't know how." She would have given a large piece of her world to have slipped into step with him. And he did not even notice what she said. All the girls were waiting to dance with him.

Once after Thankful had explained some tricky geometry to Selina, she thought that she might ask her how you knew just what step your partner was going to take, and could Selina show her. She bungled the asking, and Selina looked startled. "Oh, I couldn't show you. I don't lead. You just follow if you are a girl." Thankful thought that she had not had much practice in following. What was it her father had said she must find out? What a girl's for! If it was following, she'd never be much good at that. She did not ask Selina again.

A special dance was coming. She knew about it because Selina was chairman of the committee and could talk of nothing else. Selina was so responsible for everything that she even included Thankful. "Where would you come in," she speculated, "in a dance that seniors give freshmen? You are neither one nor the other."

"That's exactly what I am," Thankful agreed, "so I'll stay at home."

"Anyway, it's a costume party." Selina's tone made this a final point. "You know I've got an idea, Thankful." Thankful looked up hopefully. "The other day I wanted to borrow a handkerchief"—she had the grace to look embarrassed—"and I saw the cutest little plaid suit in your drawer. It seemed to be about my size—I didn't try it on." She took a hasty look at Thankful. "But why couldn't you lend it to me for the party?" She moved uneasily under Thankful's disconcerting frown. "Well, why couldn't you?"

Thankful's brows met, darkening her eyes. Gladys would have known that look. "Because I'm going to wear it myself," she said.

"Oh, well"—Selina banged out of the room—"I didn't know you were going. . . ."

Didn't myself, thought Thankful, but now I know. And if you ever touch my things again, young woman! But somehow Thankful knew that Selina wouldn't.

Thankful regretted her threat instantly. What would she do sitting around with bare knees in Robbie's Highland plaid? Robbie. Her eyes dreamed of this new Robert, so dark and smooth and finished. What would he think of her decked out in a boy's suit? Oh, well, Selina had thought well of it, and she would borrow it yet if it were still in the drawer. There was nothing to lose, Thankful thought a little drearily. Though since she was neither a freshman nor a senior, no one would expect her nor look out for her.

She was wrong. The boy called Saunders stopped her after class and asked her to go with him. "Miss Haynes told me to," he said frankly. "But as long as you don't dance you won't be any trouble."

She looked at him, fat, complacent, and decided that probably no other girl would go with him. Yet she had no choice. "Thanks," she said, "I'll try to be as little trouble as possible."

Her tone made him look up at her uneasily. "Oh, well,

you know what I mean. Getting partners, 'n' supper, 'n' things."

Thankful halted in her retreat. "You'll get me some supper," she said darkly, "or I'll know why."

"Oh, all right, all right. Meet you at eight at the gym door." He ambled down the hall, arrangements complete.

Well, anyway, she thought, I'm not afraid of Saunders. And I'd be scared to death to go with a boy—with a boy like—she couldn't quite finish even in her thoughts but Robert's face was dim in her mind. Poor Saunders, she thought, he won't like it any better than I do. But he's good-natured.

Selina laughed when she heard about Saunders, laughed until Thankful inquired dangerously, "What's so funny?"

"You! You in that queer little suit, miles taller than Fatty! You'll certainly make a funny pair." But she stopped laughing under Thankful's frown.

Just wants me to say I won't go, thought Thankful shrewdly. Well, I'll go if I only stay five minutes. The idea that she might escape early cheered her and she held to it. But she talked no more about the party to Selina. Through her casual encounters with the other girls she found out all that she wanted to know. And felt a little sick every time that she thought of it.

The early dinner Friday night she looked at palely and left. How could she ever have told Saunders that she would want supper? Perhaps she would be really sick so that there would be no question about going. But that was expecting too much of Thankful's healthy body. It would not help her out.

When she was dressed, Selina stared at her strangely between long dangling earrings. Selina was Mrs. Astor in all of the jewelry of the dormitory. She was going with a boy who would be Mrs. Astor's horse. It was a difficult part and Robert had refused it, but Selina was certain of the prize. They had practiced a good deal.

Thankful broke the short and watchful moment. "You look cute," she said honestly. "I'd never guess you were still in school!" She felt young and long and gawky. And as if a woman were staring at her. She turned uneasily to the mirror and pushed the Highland cap down over the pale hair which flew out around the edges. "I shouldn't have washed it," she said regretfully. "Do you really think"— she measured the pleated skirt with anxious eye—"do you think, Selina, that my knees show too much?"

Selina still stared. "You look all right," she said, and swept out jinglingly.

Thankful tried to see her knees in the mirror, gave it up, and put on her long coat. She would at least keep covered until she reached the gym. Funny she never felt that way before about Robbie's Highland plaid. What had possessed her to wear it! The girls were all in girls' clothes. Gypsies, nuns, queens, fairies. Would she never learn what a girl's for?

An outrageous clown leaped out at her. Saunders' voice! "Hustle up." He started in without waiting for her to take off her coat. "We got to march past the faculty. Music's beginning. I want to get near the head of the line."

"Well, I don't," said Thankful. But she had no choice. Before she had time to do more than throw her coat over a rail, Saunders without looking at her dragged her into the big hall. Laughter broke through the music. Saunders was bent on playing his part. He cavorted about her in spasms of silent mirth. And he was funny. Thankful knew it and tried to smile as he made a telescope of his hands and stared up at her Highland cap. She thought her face was frozen, and she knew that her spirit was. How could she endure the ordeal ahead of her, that endless march past staring eyes, that laughter at her, the object of a clown's fun! If floors *could* open—it must have been someone who felt like her who wished that—but the floor was waxed and hard under her feet. The procession started.

Past the grandstand of faculty. Thankful dropped her curtsey, and Saunders stood on his head. Clink, clank, she kept step when she was not pushed by Saunders. He was getting worse in his frenzy of showing off. Clink, clank, even her lips were too stiff to move into a smile anymore. She was faint with terror that tears might at any minute be running down her face. Clink, clank . . .

"Out into the middle of the hall with you, my little man! You need more room." A fine long hand placed hers on a black sleeve, and Saunders bounded away. She looked up into Mr. Fletcher's face, and then quickly down before he could see the rim of tears on her lids.

But now it was easy to swing along beside that tall figure, and the tears flowed miraculously back until she could speak and even laugh at his caustic comments. When the march broke with a clash into a fox-trot and he slipped an arm around her, terror returned. "I don't know how, I don't know how!"

"Well, you soon will," he said. "Just follow me."

She stumbled after him, and stepped on his perfect shoes, and nearly wept again. Oh, this was a party! What had possessed her to come! He was moving smoothly, firmly, as firmly as he could with her walking on him! Why couldn't she do it, too? She caught a glimpse of his suffering face.

And then suddenly she got it! She didn't know how. She didn't care. But somehow she was moving with him instead of against him, the rhythm which she had felt inside of her was outside. She could dance! At least with Mr. Fletcher. Selina with Mrs. Astor's horse passed her and stared.

The music stopped and he wiped his forehead. But he looked as pleased as Thankful felt. "It isn't as if I had to teach Latin," he said. "I could be a dancing master any moment I chose."

"You could! You certainly could!" Now the blood was

warm and fluid again in her veins. She didn't mind going home at all, and she would hurry before Saunders caught her again. "Good night, and thank you." That sounded so cold but how could she thank him? He had turned her humiliation into an accolade. Urbane, but warm, he left her. She hurried for her coat which she had left on the rail.

Turned and ran squarely into Robert, met the mischief in his face, and laughed. "Teacher's pet!" he said. "You told me you couldn't dance." The music startled her with its sudden assured attack at another dance. Robert reached for her. "Now we'll waltz," he announced.

She pulled back and he saw panic in her face. "The gal means it," he said. "Come outside and I'll show you the ropes." He led her toward the door. Better, after all, try her out first.

Robert was her own height. Their even glances crossed and she saw his impatience. It made her feel a monster of clumsiness. "I don't know where to go," she murmured desperately. "I don't know where to step."

"Ouch! Anywhere but on me," advised Robert. He backed warily off at arm's length. "Now see, it's easy. Oh, *no*! Follow me!"

But Thankful was now concentrated on dodging him, and the torture of Saunders' clowning was as play to this agony. "Please! Please!" she cried and stopped short.

Robert dropped her. "Never the twain shall meet," he

observed and stalked with her into the hall. The dance had ended and he left her with a brief "Thank you."

She sat still until the sick humiliation had drained away a little. Then she would go. "Oh, not Selina!" she cried to the approaching pair. But it was Selina, who still stared as if Thankful were something new.

"Well, you are getting rushed! My horse wants to meet you. Give him a good gallop!" and she was off with a clanking knight.

Gallop is just what I'd give him, Thankful thought bitterly. But the horse was a gentle friendly creature named Bill, and the music beat the evident rhythm of the fox-trot. Thankful was on the floor again with neither the exulting triumph of the first dance nor the devastation of the second. She was even able to ask Bill why it was that she could make her feet move in time to this beat, and not to the other.

He thought about it carefully as he guided her accurately in and out. Thankful was more wistful than she knew. Robert had ground her confidence under his proud feet. She wanted to go home but there seemed no chance to get away, and Bill was kind to her. She listened to him absently because she never really meant to try to waltz again.

"And so you see," he ended, "just how easy it is."

Thankful sighed and thought that she might have paid attention.

"Because," he went on, "you are doing it exactly as I told you."

Thankful's startled look made him laugh. "For the last few minutes you have been waltzing unusually well. You never noticed when the time shifted. You just followed." He smiled gently at her through his spectacles which looked odd in his horse head. "You're all set now." He motioned to a sandy-haired ruddy boy. "Hey, MacFarland, here's a Scotch lassie you'd like." She hoped that the horse would get the prize.

From that springboard, she slipped into the evening as easily as if it had always been her medium. Her plaid kilt swished among the gay skirts, and she forgot her bare knees, and perplexity of where your partner would step next. Angus MacFarland hadn't known that there was a Scotch girl in school. "And can you do the Highland fling?" She could, and they tapped out a few steps together in a corner. That was the best of all.

Even Saunders was subdued by suppertime. His activity had so filled him with hunger that he had small attention for Thankful's plate. But she had eaten no dinner and endured much since, so that she kept him busy. He disappeared when Mr. Fletcher sauntered up with an extra plate of ice cream for Thankful.

"I got so hungry!" Thankful apologetically finished the cream while he watched in companionable silence. "And I had such fun!"

"Good for you!" he applauded. "As far as dancing is concerned you're a natural."

Thankful thought bitterly of her struggle with Robert. Nothing could sweeten that tragedy. Though he had passed her many times he had looked away in blank indifference. What must he have thought of her clumsy failure with him who was, Selina said, the perfect partner. He would never ask her again. But Mr. Fletcher was talking to her.

"I like the Highland fling," he observed.

"So do I," agreed Thankful.

"You wouldn't like to give us a bit of it after supper if I can stir up the music?" He lifted a sardonic eyebrow at her start. "I saw you jigging it up in the corner."

The color crept over her face. What would this evening demand of her next! All the pleasure in it had come through his help. She couldn't refuse him but she was so terrified that she could not remember even the first step of the fling.

"Probably they don't know the tune," she suggested hopefully.

"They said they did."

Silence. She looked up at him desperately and he smiled. An engaging smile! She stared at the floor, her lashes dark on her cheek.

"Could Angus MacFarland do it with me?"

He beckoned to Angus who rose at once. The chattering room was more aware of her corner than Thankful knew. Angus said politely that he would be glad to help out if he had a plaid, but that a fellow would look a fool dancing the fling in a baseball costume.

Thankful wanted to disagree with him but she couldn't.

Angus went back to his table. Silence again. Then a small voice, "I would but I can't seem to remember how it goes."

The man rose. "They're all going back now. Let's get it over with."

Thankful stole a look at him. He was implacable. Now why, she thought angrily, must he spoil what fun I've had! He knows I have to do what he says. He knows I hate it. She caught Robert's cold glance in her unwilling progress toward the orchestra, and moaned under her breath at what he must witness now. Not one step could she remember.

The leader, who had bent over the edge of the platform to hear Mr. Fletcher, straightened up, and lifted his stick. Poised couples waited for the first note, and stopped hesitant at the odd scrape of the violins. Only a few of the musicians could handle it, and they needed a moment of practice. Selina, the chairman, bustled up. "What *is* this dance?" And Mr. Fletcher waved her away politely. Now they had it! That inimitable sharp scrape which only the pipes could really sound.

Angus, well forward where Thankful could see him, shuffled his feet encouragingly into the first steps. Oh, yes, it went that way, but her feet were iron shod. The leader turned. "Now!" he shouted, and startled, Thankful sprang into the dance.

Forget the Highland fling? Forget how to breathe! She and her brothers dancing on the grass. Mother's old accordion. The floorboards of the attic shaking under her feet. Robbie's kilts flying, hair flying, spirits flying! The tune blew the wind from over the sea, cold and bright. Her feet were as light as its touch.

The scraping bows ground down to the end. And down came Thankful's arms, her uplifted chin, her flying hair. What a queer thing the old tune had done to her! She felt alone and bleak now that it had stopped. The noise! The noise! "Could I go now?" Nobody could hear her and she went. Confused and uncomfortable under the beating applause. And filled with such homesickness as she had not known yet. This night had been too much!

Two more dances with boys cutting in, and the party was over. Her coat was still on the rail, but astoundingly Saunders held it for her. "Made quite a hit, didn't you?" She hardly heard his patter. She ached as she had after she left the island. This night had been too much!

A vague sense of Selina, uncommunicative. Now, what have I done to *her*? Weary groping, with no solution. And Robert's friendliness gone too. It *was* a party!

Then against the dun quiet of her drowsy lids she saw faces pressing against her, interested, aware. Boys, girls, even those men and women on the platform. Looking at her as she shrank away from them. Yet seeing her, seeing her, she suddenly realized, for the first time. And then so sharply that it cut down deep into her sleep and brought her sitting up to the stars outside her window, she knew why Mr. Fletcher had made her do this thing. She was no longer a shadow! She lay down and slept the profound sleep of the tired young.

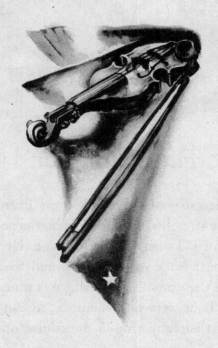

False Summer

The Indian summer sun lay soft on Thankful's eye-
lids. She stretched into comfort on the pebbly beach
and waited for old man Dinkle to come. He was going
to haul up next week so that she would have no more
Saturdays on the water. She knew it was time. This pale
sea and soft light were false summer. Already they had
twice fought their way around the course on Saturdays

when the fall wind had whipped the bay feather white. She knew, but she could not face the procession of weeks ahead when no shining day barred off each end.

Still there was today. The sun poured over and soaked into her, but without much heat. Winter was coming. She heard fewer crickets now in the harsh grass, and the bayberry twigs were stiff with dull blue clusters. The berries had been jade green when she left Bright Island.

It was curious, she thought, how Bright Island never left her. Always the feeling of it was in her senses, apple green of the sky, the taste of its fog on her lips, its lovely quiet. She knew now that she would never be tuned to the noise of many people. That she would always be troubled by their strange ways.

She sighed deeply as she thought of Robert and Selina. Since that dance they had dropped her entirely. When Selina had said, "Well, you had a swell time showing off, didn't you?" Thankful had slashed back against her hurt. And then there had been quiet between them, but not the peace of this quiet in the sun. An ugly stillness. The kind that brooded before a storm broke. Thankful had never known it between humans before.

Robert she understood better. Boys were easier to understand. He was so gay, so irresponsible. He valued people who gave him a good time. She had failed him at that dreadful dance, had touched his vanity. Probably he thought that she showed off, too. Queer what

Robbie's plaid had done for her that night. She could hear now Robert's voice, "Gal, where've you kept all those good looks!" and she saw Selina's staring woman's eyes. Anyway, she rolled over and felt the freedom of her overalls—she was part of the rest of the school now. Though even they looked at her puzzled sometimes as if trying to reconcile two different people. It was those dreadful clothes that the girls had bought her. She wished that the tide would carry away the dress which she had tucked behind a rock when she put on her overalls.

Those overalls! She had had them on last week when Mr. Fletcher suddenly appeared on the beach. The gloom left her as she thought of last week and she felt light and comfortable again. She and old Dinkle had been busily loading the dinghy when there he was, leaning against a rock.

"Hullo," he said, and "Hullo," they both said.

"So you do have some fun, don't you?" He came up to the boat and handed Dinkle the oars. Thankful had introduced them as well as she could with old Dinkle shoving the boat. Mr. Fletcher took hold, too, and they got it to the water's edge in no time.

"Have a good haul," he said and he managed to look wistful.

Old Dinkle held the dinghy back with an oar. "Want to come, young feller?" Just as if he had been one of the boys. Robert, if Robert could be imagined there! And without waiting to answer, he had given the bow a push and leaped aboard. He had on old clothes, too, though they didn't look like Dinkle's.

Dinkle asked him what his name was, though Thankful had already told him. Orin Fletcher. And if the old man didn't call him Orin! Just as if he had been one of the boys. So easily that Thankful did it herself once. She turned scarlet now as she thought of it. He had started to cast off too soon and she had shouted from the wheel, "Hold her, Orin, hold her!" She was glad he hadn't noticed it and was very careful after that. But curiously enough she found herself thinking of him as the old man called him, Orin with the first letter drawled a little. Perhaps it was because on an island you called people quite simply by their own names. She sighed. There she was back to the island again.

But it had been easy to talk about Bright Island that day. Not while they were hauling, though that was fun too. He had been so quick in his motions that Dinkle said he was through before he had begun. And Thankful had to show him how to do so many things that she entirely forgot that he was usually the teacher. He seemed to forget it too, and they laughed a great deal over his mistakes.

It was while they had their snack that they talked so much about Bright Island. Thankful was surprised when she remembered how much she had told him. Luckily he had a sandwich of his own, and a whole pocket full of chocolate bars. Old Dinkle had relished those! Thankful hardly got one for herself, and she didn't see Orin—Mr. Fletcher—eat a single one.

As Thankful lay there on the beach and recalled the fun they had had, it seemed surprisingly the best trip yet. If she had considered beforehand including someone who was so Latin-wise, she would have been sure of a spoiled day. But he really had added something which she couldn't quite define. The day seemed saltier, with more flavor. Fuller of laughter, and quick gay talk. Not once his sardonic tongue.

Thankful sprang to her feet and ran to help old man Dinkle slithering over the beach grass with his mended spray hood. "May need it before we get 'em hauled today," he grunted, and Thankful nodded, wise to the November sea.

Before he shoved off, the old man squinted up and down the shore. "Orin comin'?" he asked.

Thankful had looked, too. "I guess not," she said. "He might think he was pushing himself in."

"Good comp'ny." Dinkle pulled short hard strokes to his powerboat. "Good choc'let."

Thankful reached in the pocket of her jeans. "I brought you some."

Dinkle's eyes gleamed under bushy brows. "Might try a chaw when we get her off," he said.

The powerboat chugged smoothly out of the cove

with Thankful at the wheel. She knew the location of each lobster pot now. But today instead of rebaiting the slatted cage and dropping it back again, Dinkle piled the pots neatly in the bow. As they putted briskly around the next point he cocked a withered eye toward the shore.

"That fool sloop goin' out today? Should 'a' been hauled up two weeks ago."

Thankful didn't want her happiness spoiled. This last day. They had passed her in a car, Robert and Selina. No bus when his boat had been ordered up the first of the month. Selina had hired the car because Robert was always broke, and it was one way to make him take her sailing. Thankful had heard all this gossip from the girls, but she didn't want to think about it now. Her thoughts must leave them alone, and the clean white sloop, and their lunch together on an island. If she could but set foot on an island again, a wild sweet-smelling island! She swung the wheel and slid up to a bobbing buoy. It was enough to be out with the gulls this morning. They swirled and shrieked after the discarded bait. She thought of Limpy, strong and free. And Dave! She missed Dave suddenly, and then forgot him. Robert's brown hair smooth and close to his head, Robert's quick grace, oh, she wished that Robert would keep out of her thoughts! She wanted all of them for this last day on the water. Where was her pride to let them wander away to those young people who had no thought of her? The sloop fell behind the wooded point and she whistled urgently to her sad heart.

She and Dinkle had a companionable snack none the less appetizing from the smell of dead herring which hung over the boat. Not even a crust for the screaming gulls who followed to the last haul. Some pots must be left for another trip but now there was work enough to stow these into the shed above the tide line. Back and forth they trudged from the beached boat, the old man strong and gnarled, the girl young and straight in her faded jeans. One on each side until the last pot was piled away for the winter.

Out at the mooring old Dinkle fastened down the spray hood. "Blow before night," he said, and they jogged their heads together at the piled ranks of wind clouds in the north. "Spell o' weather on the way. Hope that fool boy'll haul up his sloop now."

Robert back again in her thoughts when she just cleared him away. He must have come in long ago. It was late. Stacking the pots had taken so long. She must run. It was good-bye then. And "Come a good day in March, we'll get her off again." March. Months away. So long to wait! And then she remembered that when March came she would be only two months from Bright Island and she ran with swift glad steps as if toward that time. The old man plodded through the pasture without looking ahead or behind.

At the turn of the road where the coastline stretched

to either side, Thankful paused and looked. Looked again, and then again to be sure. Robert's boat was not at its mooring. Then she remembered with a quick lift of her breath that he might have sailed it down to the yard where it was to be hauled up for the winter. Of course, she thought. Of course he did. He wouldn't want them to know up at school that his boat was still out. Though she knew how little he cared in his gay insubordination, and how gentle with him the authorities were. "Spoiled, he is," she said, and then she saw the car still braked in the beach grass. Robert and Selina becalmed out there somewhere were waiting for those black rolling clouds to bring them wind. And they little knew how much, she thought grimly.

It was curious how much she knew of their plans in spite of the indifference she had worked so hard to achieve. A sail to Hogback, a swim, a driftwood fire, steak, marshmallows—a stolen picnic which no one would permit; and stolen, all the better. But what if this escapade ended other than they planned? Thankful could already see the whitecaps edging the outer bars. A November nor'wester was too strong medicine for that little boat. She was built for summer seas.

A slap of wind, chilled as if from the bottom of the sea, struck her sharply. She shivered down into her sweater though not from cold. Best wait around a few minutes, she thought. They'll be right in now the breeze has come up. She hated to get back to school late. Miss Haynes let her have these Saturdays knowing her need, and that she would be back on time. Thankful could not bear to worry her. But, she thought, swallowing her pride, I'll ride up in their car and save time. I must be sure about them.

The wind clouds swept low now and helped to darken the brief November day. Thankful watched the water ruffle and break into gray fragments under them. Not too squally, she thought, they could weather this. Hope they've plenty of warm clothes. But she had seen Selina dress in her smart linen slacks and shirt, and the coat she wore to cover them was slung across the car seat.

Why didn't they hurry? Didn't they *know*—know what, that the day was darkening, that the wind from those overhanging clouds could break them, that she was waiting, oh, what could she do if that small boat did not sail around the point soon!

Across the road the ground rose in a brief knoll which might overlook the wooded point. Thankful pulled herself up through wild rose brambles which tore at her, into alder brush, and out on the flat granite top. There it was! Flitting over the dark water toward her like a small pale moth. The relief was so sharp that it hurt. She was consumed with anger toward that pair for the anguish they had caused her. Let them make their mooring as they could! She would run for it now and reach the campus as soon as they did.

The sloop went about, tacking close into the wind. Thankful stopped short at the edge of the rocky summit. "The fool! The fool!" she cried. "Why don't you reef your sail!" Her voice blew back into her throat. All sail on to make time, and no thought about consequences. She knew, she knew what Robert would do. She could see his dark figure bent over the wheel, and a crouched huddle of white which spelled Selina. Were they frightened? Reckless, reckless lad to pay no heed to that wild wind! It blew her hair into her eyes and she pushed the pale mop back and peered distractedly under her hands.

The sail from her knoll looked almost flat on the water. Selina, backed against the rail, was braced erect now. The sloop shoved itself nose deep through choppy waves rushing crazily at each other. Its keel was bare. "The good little boat! The good little boat!" Thankful cried to it watching it wallow. "You can make it! Oh, if he'd only reefed her! Robert! Robert!" she screamed. "Robert! Head her up! Head her up!" and then she was running, running blindly, purposefully, through brush and brambles. The sloop had capsized.

Her feet took no caution that she knew, but they bore her sure and swift as wings. Down to the road, up the shore, to the dinghy pulled high from the tide. Dragging, tugging at the heavy stern, until waves crashed over its edge. Her breath stopped in her throat now, and she panted like a dog. Into the water beside the boat until it cleared the chop, and then over the side, and pull, pull, pull. Almost as much water inside as out. But nothing could sink that dory. Oh, could those two hold on until she got there! Could she hurry any faster! If she could only breathe!

She leaped aboard the powerboat, and flung the dory's loop over the mooring pole. Here, here in the diddy box he kept the key. Dave had always rolled up the wheel. She thought of Dave now. She knew how, but she had no breath. And if it would not catch! Oh, she couldn't think of that—she reached down and gave it a mighty roll.

It caught! And she flung herself against the tiller. Broadside she must run, no easing her off. Robert and Selina struggling in that icy water, clutching at a slippery keel—oh, hold on! Hold on! I'm coming. If she could ever get beyond the point where she could see if—where she could see if—she pushed back what she might have to see. Her breath was easier now, and she felt every elastic muscle stretch and pull at the boat's speed. It was so slow! When the motor coughed once she felt sick and faint.

She took a chance at rocks and cut close to the point. Around it, leaning out to prick into the space ahead. In the gloom, nothing. Nothing but crazy fighting waves. Thankful moaned, pushing hopelessly on. Then her terror found voice and she heard herself above the wind screaming their names. "Where are you! Where are you! I'm coming!" If the wind would be quiet to let her hear.

She was almost on them when she saw them, Selina lurched over the flattened rudder, Robert hanging to the bowsprit. Water dashing over them and the flat white sail. Instantly Thankful felt her wild pulses quiet. They were here, and she could get them. Calm and sure, she slid at low speed as near as she dared.

"Catch!" She hurled one of the ropes old Dinkle had used to tie his lobster pots together. It curled over the half-sunk bowsprit and into Robert's numb fingers. He made a clumsy hitch and cried hoarsely, "Hurry!"

Her arms, her heart, pulled her toward him first. Robert. He could so easily slip now! His poor stiff hands— but Selina *was* slipping. A limp, huddled heap. Thankful dragged at her rope, drifted closer, grabbed at the white slacks, and Selina had tumbled into the bottom of the powerboat. Thankful could hear her gasping, "Oh, I'm so thankful, thankful, thankful," and thought she was calling her. But she had no more heed for Selina.

Robert tried valiantly to help her, but she thought that she had lost him twice. Somehow he caught the rope each time he fell, but the waves dashed over his white drowned face and Thankful thought he must let go. She talked, talked, talked to him. Not that he could hear her words. But her steadying voice, her set determined face swaying above him, her strong young arms, finally they got him aboard. He rolled down beside the engine and was very sick. She thought, perhaps he will mind this most of all, and looked sharp for a chance to free their mooring to the wreck.

She was still enough of a sailor to feel that she cut away something alive. But there was no more that she could do for the sloop. It would wash ashore, and with luck it would make the sheltered cove. They would come down tomorrow and retrieve it. Thankful swung out in an arc until, the wind behind her, she leaped with the waves toward the mooring where the dinghy bumped.

Bitten to the skin by the icy spray, the cold wind pouring over her wet body, Thankful still was conscious only of a warm core that could not be reached. Down there, cowering close to the engine box in the lee of the gale, were two live people. Wretched, half frozen, water streaming from them, Selina sobbing and Robert ghastly with shut eyes, yet there! Alive and—she held the dinghy with one hand and pushed them into it with the other—almost ashore.

No one could help her pull the dory back above high water except the tide which was at the full. I'll give it an extra hist tomorrow, she promised herself. She measured the task ahead of her. How to get this numb stumbling pair as far as the car. They waited for her to decide, motionless where she had dragged them from the dinghy. She could not manage both of them at once.

"Robert, you come with me and we'll drive back for Selina." Oh, if she only could drive that car! Would Robert? It would take so long for her to run back to the school for help. They would freeze down here waiting. "Robert!" She spoke more sharply. "Come along with me. Exercise will warm you best."

He stood dripping and looked at her vaguely. Her heart was wrung. "Come on." She seized his arm and propelled him toward the road. Selina moaned, "Don't leave me," but no one noticed her. His feet slipped back over the loose pebbles and she could see his knees begin to fold. She thrust a strong tired arm around him and hoisted him over the bank to the road. How slight and fine he felt!

"Now faster, just a little jog trot, see like this," she urged and prodded until she could feel his muscles under her arm come to life. She thought there had never been a piece of road so long. Then she could see the car settled down into the gloom of the dark beach grass.

"Can't drive it," Robert muttered. The car smelled stuffy and warm. Robert folded his arms over the wheel and rested his wet dark head on them. Thankful could have cried.

"That's perfect blethers!" Her mother always broke into Scotch when she scolded. "I cannot abide such softness. Pick up your head off that wheel."

Robert raised startled eyes, and she met them with her dark-browed frown. "Now get on with you." She was relentless in her need. "We'll not leave Selina to chill on the beach. You can go that far, and if need be I'll run it the rest." She watched his shaking hands start the car, and kept a hand on the wheel as it swerved down the road. "It's not unlike enough to a boat to bother," she said. "You can leave the steering to me. Though I don't know as I can bring her around."

The turn was a problem and the car sheered crazily about the road before it faced home. But Selina was aboard and Robert was still at the wheel. At the gate he pushed Thankful's hand from the wheel. "I'll take it in," he said shortly. She thought, he is remembering now the hard words I said to him. Oh, Robert! But because his hand was steady she let him go.

There could be nothing secret about this return. Through the lighted windows of the dining room their empty places proclaimed them. Thankful saw the great roast, and hunger brought her first weakness. She trembled as she watched the maid bear it away for the dessert. Suddenly she felt the sorrows of the world bear down upon her, and she wept. This last straw had broken her.

Robert was ready to dominate again. She heard his voice running on to Miss Haynes. But she did not care what he said. The lost roast stood for a spar which would have saved her from drowning. She crept up to her room and dropped her wet clothes on the floor while Edie helped Selina into bed.

Edie left them and went out. Thankful crawled shivering under the blankets. The wind and the fear and her hunger had beaten her down. She seemed hollowed into the bed, flat and lifeless. Her hair dried in wisps on the pillow, her lashes were feather dark. She felt that nothing could rouse her again.

Edie held the door back with her foot and pushed her way in. The curling smell of hot roast beef woke Thankful's tired senses. Edie set the tray down between the beds. "Want I should feed you?" she asked. Selina moaned assent. Thankful sat up briskly. She took the loaded plate from Edie and silently set to work. Through the roast and vegetables while Selina fussed over a glass of hot milk. But before the last spoonful of ice cream was reached, she slid back on the pillows with the soft breathing of untroubled sleep.

PART III

Bright Island Now and Then

Bright Island Thanksgiving

Thankful was puzzled by Selina. Her pride made her wary of the girl's advances. She mustn't feel that she has to be nice to me, Thankful thought, just because I happened to haul her out of the water that day. Anybody would have. And I'm no different now than I was before.

But Selina persisted. She seemed softened and humbled. She invited Thankful to do this and that, and brought her little gifts of sweets which she offered tentatively as if she feared refusal. Thankful ate the candy, but withheld her affection. In these months she had built up a resistance against Selina which was not easily brought low. It had helped her to stand the daily hurts and it still held her unresponsive behind its protection. Selina met with unexpected rebuff.

To Thankful's embarrassment the school treated her as its hero for nearly a week. When they had forgotten the reason for their conduct, they still kept shreds of the new pattern toward her. Thankful had no lack of companionship these days. Indeed, with the Dinkle Saturdays gone she felt a desperate need sometimes to escape what she called their yammer and yawl. She liked them but the need of healing quiet was her island heritage.

When a letter from her mother proposed Thanksgiving day at home, she sat over it mute with joy while Selina chattered words which she did not hear. Jed had to come up the coast the day before and he would bring her over in his powerboat. Her father would take her back the next day. Mary Curtis was brief but she made it possible for her daughter to come home. Bring someone with you if you wish, she had added in a postscript, but Thankful paid it no heed. She was going home to Bright Island. She would see it brown and bare in the November desolation which she loved. She would lie under the eaves in her cold little room, and look out at stars higher and in great numbers.

She would hear the plash of the small waves in the cove, and smell their saltiness, clean, unbreathed.

She drew a long deep breath as if to catch their scent and looked up from the page in her hand to find Selina staring at her. "Someone just left you a diamond ring?" she asked with familiar tartness.

Thankful folded up her letter. "Best one I ever had." She kept herself absent from Selina. It was the only way to do.

Selina made a queer noise in her throat. Then the words tumbled by her anger. "You make me mad! You never tell me anything. I run on and on, and all you ever do in return is to shut up tight and leave me guessing. You just keep yourself to yourself."

Thankful's astonished eyes watched her. Does she think I want her to go on and on? Doesn't she know how I have to stop listening? Does she want me to tell her about me? She flinched under the impact of this idea. Keep yourself to yourself? Of course, or not keep it at all! But Selina wouldn't understand that.

"It's only a letter from home," she said gently. After all, Selina seemed to be trying for friendliness after these hard weeks. "I didn't know you'd be interested."

Selina's flares of anger were always brief. "Well. I'm not, really. But I'd just like to have you tell me."

"Oh. Well, I got a letter from home and I'm going back to Bright Island for Thanksgiving." Even telling it made her eyes shine again.

151

Selina tried to prove how much she appreciated this confidence. Each day the island Thanksgiving increased its glamor in her imagination. Thankful's happiness and Selina's urge produced details which Selina seized and nursed. Thankful didn't mind. It was a special day at Bright Island, a festivity, not a sharing of her real life there. And her talk about it stopped Selina's incessant mourning that the school did not allow time for her to go home. Thankful forgot her weather-wise ways and paid too little heed as to how the wind was blowing until it was too late for her to change her course. Selina would not let her go about!

Thankful hardly knew how it happened when she thought it over in cold despair. She had been absently sympathetic. Ready and waiting an hour early for the bus. "Too bad you can't go home. I wish you could . . ."

And then the interruption of swift words seizing upon her unfinished sentence, giving it astounding significance. "Oh, Thankful, I could! I'd love to! You don't know how I hoped you'd ask me! Oh, won't we have fun!" and an ecstatic hug.

Thankful stared over Selina's shoulder at the wall. What had she done? Her day at Bright Island shattered by her own clumsy motion. Selina knew, she must know how little Thankful wanted her. What had she said? She couldn't remember, and as she thought about it, Selina's excitement covered her stony silence. She already had her

152

suitcase out of the closet and was plunging about in her search for proper clothes. I'll have to stop her! I'll have to tell her! "Selina!" but Selina had disappeared.

In a moment she was back with Miss Haynes. "Of course, Thankful. I am so glad that you invited Selina to go with you. I'll help her to get ready. You run down to the door and hold the bus."

No time to notice her stricken face. No chance given her to escape. She had a moment's desperate plan to leap into the bus and hurry it away. But after all, Mary Curtis had brought her up.

When Selina flung herself and her suitcase into the bus Thankful had settled herself into its corner, curiously white and grave for one who was off on a holiday. Selina was so busy trying to make Robert wave to her that she had no attention for Thankful's pallor.

"He's so queer nowadays." She flounced down beside Thankful. "Ever since he wrecked me on his old boat, he's been offish."

"Is that so?" murmured Thankful.

"Yes, it's so. And what's more, he can't seem to talk about anybody but you." Her anger started to flare, sputtered out under sudden recollection of her new relation to Thankful. "He was crazy to come too."

Thankful felt the first small flicker of something alive since she had killed her island holiday. Robert thought about her. That he envied Selina was beyond her belief, but she had a swift vision of him on her island with her in the places she cherished. Ah, that would be a Thanksgiving.

She turned toward Selina, suddenly warm again. "That fur coat will feel good on the boat," she said. "Jed has a cabin but I always like to sit out on deck. He'll bring my slicker." And at the thought of Jed bringing her slicker, and the boat rushing through the waves to Bright Island, her heart began to sing. Underneath the song was Robert.

Jed liked Selina and tucked her up in the warm shelter of the cabin. He and Thankful sat together by the wheel in companionable silence. She thought she might never have been away. The spray stung color back into her face and felt cold and right on her bare hands. Bright Island came up over the horizon and gleamed through her wet lashes with rainbow radiance. "The spray," she muttered and rubbed them dry that she might miss no small detail.

There it lay, this outer island which held all her heart, blue water touching it, blue sky hanging over it, and the silver-gray house at its edge. There was in the whole world never anything so lovely.

Mary Curtis flung open the kitchen door, waved, and disappeared. Then Thankful knew that something had gone into the oven, and suddenly she was hungry. The door flew open again and her mother ran down the beach. Thankful's spirit rushed over the water but her hands somehow helped Jed. So slow, so slow he was! She longed for a swift dive and swim ashore. She forgot Selina until she heard her in a small helpless voice, "I'm scared of small boats since the wreck. Please help me," and Jed helped her carefully into the dinghy.

Click, click, the oars, and Thankful in the stern, the forward cant of her body pushing them on. A long leap when the pebbles grated, and Bright Island was under her feet. In the low afternoon sun it lay in the peace she remembered. It took her home again.

Selina had to be introduced to her mother, hospitable, friendly, to her father, stiff and shy, to the house though she didn't know it, to all of Bright Island that she could see. Thankful found sudden relief from too great pressure in whisking Selina about. She saw her mother's amused glance and remembered her exact tone, "She'll chitter like a finch when she's lived with the girls awhile." Never mind! Never mind! She fought on against the choke in her throat which no one must know.

She could see Selina's eyes wander about the rooms. They did look curiously small after those high square rooms. But sweet, sweet. The shabby comfortable chairs, her mother's books, the old table polished to a golden patina by a hundred years of use, the Franklin stove which filled the summer fireplace, these things that she had always known touched her deeply with their familiar sweetness. Like Bright Island, they took her back. No one knew about that. The talk ran on.

Then just as the lamps were lighted, she could leave
Selina contentedly unpacking in the boys' old room. She
could leave her mother stirring up biscuits in the kitchen
spicy with warm gingerbread, neat, yet full of the business of living. She could leave her father with less ease
than anyone because he somehow followed her about. She
could run through the cold purple of the twilight, up the
path past the pale gravestones settled into the sleeping
earth, up and out until the whole island lay beneath her.
She stood still under the slow lighting stars and waited.
One by one like the things in the house, they came home
to her, the darkening mountains, the darkened sea, the
brown sweet fern pasture, speared with pointed trees
which brushed her knees, they all came gently, quietly,
home to her. When she had hailed them all, she raced
back to the lighted house, the clean island air sharp in her
nostrils.

The stock and the chickens were housed for the night,
yet in the empty henyard Thankful could see the white
outline of a great bird moving gravely about with bobbing
head. "Limpy!" she called. "Limpy! You beggar!" And the
gull rose on wide wings, circled over her head, and slipped
effortlessly into the darkness. Her mother laughed when
Thankful told her. "He came the first cold spell," she said.
"He gets handouts from the hens. You have to learn to
work when you're young."

Thankful set the table with Selina dodging at her

heels to see how she did it. "I shall help tomorrow for the Thanksgiving dinner," she promised. "I learn quickly."

She did, Thankful realized. She was at home with Mary and Jonathan Curtis, coaxing them, laughing with them, admiring them with her eyes. Thankful wondered at her quick adjustment, and for the first time found a clue to her popularity at school. She despaired at the certainty of what she would have been in Selina's family. They could not have found anyone more different than Selina to room with her, she thought, and felt respect for Selina's difficulties with her. How pretty she was in that simple little dress which Thankful knew had cost more than her whole outfit! Selina told her. Yet Selina did not measure all her values by money. Look at her now, her face gentle in the lamplight, liking their homely supper, eating largely of it. And talking, talking, talking. Her mother and father liked the chatter and Jed had liked it and wished that he could stay to hear more. Thankful began to have a discouraged sense about herself as a daughter.

But when her mother had lighted them upstairs, and settled Selina for the night, she sat on Thankful's bed a moment. "She's a bonny lass"—she nodded toward the boys' old room—"but too gabby for steady living." She rose and blew out the light. "I like my own girl," she said into the darkness.

The door shut and Thankful sat up in bed. For a moment the stars blurred, but she felt very comfortable.

With a queer kind of satisfaction, too, as if for the first time she had been measured against another and not fallen too far short. It was almost worth bringing Selina home for, she thought, and curled softly down under the warm blankets. The day had been mild for November, but the night had a sharp edge. Selina would be glad of those heated bricks. She felt hers, stretching her length, and touching their warmth fell asleep.

Then suddenly it was morning and Thankful woke to watch blue smoke ascend to blue sky over the kitchen ell. Another mild day, a last breath of fall. A day such as seldom came to the island so late. Warm enough for open windows to let the smell of roasting turkey reach almost to the shore. To make it certain that all the boys and their wives could come over from the mainland. Though that was no advantage, Thankful thought.

She dreaded the girls for Selina almost as she did for herself. She dreaded them so deeply that she could find small room to be glad at the news that Dave would be with them. He always came for Thanksgiving. Yet when Jed's big boat chugged around the point it was the sight of Dave in the bow waiting to catch the mooring that made the flutter and fuss of the girls bearable. Thankful sprang for her father's old peapod and pushed out. It always took two boatloads to bring them all ashore.

But her boat filled up with fuss and flutter before Dave could leave Jed, before he had time to do more than tweak her hair as he helped Gladys aboard. She ducked under his big hand and shoved her peapod away, looking back at him in his uniform.

"Aye, what a bonny lad! All in his blue kilties!" She dodged a sponge which leaped from Ethel's lap to the water where it sank. Ethel brushed and rubbed all the way ashore. He'll catch it, Thankful thought pleasurably.

But when Dave made his stiff little bow to Selina, even Thankful could not believe it an intentional sponge. And Ethel said no more about it. The sponge had left no impression comparable with Selina. Pretty as a late dandelion with the sun shining on her yellow dress and yellow hair. They stood around her on the beach and warmed to her, the girls saying this and that in high voices to get her attention. Thankful thought that she could see Dave now and turned to find his eyes on Selina. He was bigger, and—aye, he *was* a bonny lad! She felt dowdy and dark in her thick wool and hurried up the beach to help her mother.

A scuffle of heavy shoes on the pebbles and Dave was beside her, hurrying too. "Did you see where your sponge landed?" She would not look at the beautiful uniform.

But Dave was sniffing the air. "Turkey!" he moaned. "Oh, smell that turkey! Couldn't we chop the giblets for the gravy, Thankful?" And they were all right again. Mary Curtis always let them chop the giblets. And if they took toll, after all the gravy shouldn't be too rich for those girls.

Over the giblets Thankful heard what she wanted to know about the cutter, and Dave's work on her, and how he managed to change his day off with an officer who had no folks near here, and soon the ice breaking would begin. . . .

"Break us out here on the island?" inquired Mary Curtis.

"Keep you open all winter," boasted Dave.

"Dar'st I come home Christmas?" Thankful stopped nibbling.

"Come home as easy as if a train ran out here. Could bring Selina along, too. I'll see you out."

"Oh. Well, Selina goes home herself at Christmas. Guess you'd have to put up with me," and was sorry she said it.

Dave grinned. "Done that quite awhile."

Mrs. Curtis removed the giblet bowl. "Need a wee taste for the gravy."

The two sauntered regretfully away.

It was a dinner such as only Mary Curtis could prepare with her unhurried competence. No soup, no fish, nothing to take the edge off the great golden bird which she carved herself. Jonathan had refused years ago to touch the Thanksgiving turkey. The management of its details required too fine a technique. Her own herbs, thyme, savory, sage, seasoned the stuffing. Her own cranberries gathered from the lower bog furnished the sweet tart sauce. Winter squash steamed soft and mashed into golden pulp with homemade butter. The late white turnips beaten into mildness with fresh cream. Onions clean stripped and full flavored with only butter and salt to keep their racy taste. No flour sauces here to dilute good food, Mary Curtis always said. And never had she offered them a more appetizing dinner.

As ever, after her first sharp appetite, Thankful begrudged the long hours crowded under a roof. The girls, she decided, were worse than ever. They ate with fingers crooked, and spoke of the food with high artificial voices, asking Selina about this and that in the school. Dave listened gravely, and Thankful saw that his eyes were always on Selina. To her surprise she heard fine things about herself. It seemed that they had not understood she could finish in one year. Her mother looked startled, and then proud. Dave threw her a swift glance and then attended to Selina again. He seemed hungry to hear all that she could say. Thankful cared nothing for their praise, she surprisingly discovered. She wanted to get away.

But Mary Curtis had baked mince pies, and steamed a plum pudding with hard sauce stung with sherry, and she was firm about them both. "You get nothing like this at school," she said. "Now eat."

Selina reproached her. "I should say we didn't! I never got anything like it anywhere!"

Dave shot her a sudden smile. Thankful couldn't tell what it meant. But she realized resentfully that he was in no hurry to leave the table. Nor was Selina. She charmed them all by counting on her manicured fingers, Mr. Curtis, Mrs. Curtis, Mr. Curtis, Mrs. Curtis, all the way around the table with only a provocative look at Dave. Then back again, Mr. Jed, Mrs. Ethel, Mr. Silas, Mrs. Gladys, she had every name right and a smile for each. "Please," she said, "you are not alike and I can't call you all by the same name." Thankful could feel the flattery warm them by its personal salute. Dave looked left out, and she grinned. He caught it out of the corner of his eye.

The girls washed the dishes as usual, and then they must go, days so short now, children be back from granny's, such a good dinner Mother Curtis, good-bye Selina, pleased to meet you, come over to see us sometime, Thankful, the school is doing you good. A touching little-girl eagerness to please about them. Then they were gone. Leaving behind them as always the heightened awareness of peace and quiet. Even Selina felt it and yawned quietly in a corner. Thankful left her and caught what remained of the sweet mild day.

They had stirred confusion in her mind as ever. A need to find that quiet core of herself again. Even Dave—she was a little homesick for Dave with his absorption in Selina. Though she could still feel the quick hard grasp of his hand when he left her. She sighed and dismissed him with the rest. Only a few more hours now and she must leave Bright Island. Why spend the time thinking about people! She pushed through the brown pastures, down into the pointed wood, and out on the bare headland where the waves whished and plashed on the mildest day. Going on and on like this ever since she had left them. They made her feel stretched out, part of something greater than she, unharassed. She stayed there until it was quite dark and she had to feel her way back through the wood.

That night Mary Curtis brought her lamp into Thankful's room and sat down in the rocker. "There's no reason I can see," she announced to Thankful, half asleep, "why you shouldn't look as well as the best." Thankful woke up.

Her mother wasted no words. "Something is altogether wrong with those clothes. You'll get yourself new ones." She interrupted Thankful's expostulation. "If it's money you're thinking of, you've enough. Gramp left you two years of schooling. You've need of but one." She made an effort not to look proud. "I'll see that you can put your hands on enough for clothes to suit you. The girls did what they could," she apologized, rising, "but best get Selina to help you this time." She unexpectedly bent over and kissed Thankful.

The morning was dank. A raw wind swept up the bay and blew clouds over the mountains. No day for Jonathan's open boat and he knew it. Even Mary Curtis could not lighten the gloom of the early breakfast. "Got to get off, haven't I?" he grumbled at her. "So's to get back."

Thankful felt like the morning. Not one glint of light anywhere. Except that Dave had said she could make it at Christmas. And even he had offered so that she could bring Selina. Well, she wouldn't, but she'd come herself. The island crouched low and wet when she looked back at it, as if it didn't care either. Selina moped. She had eaten too much of the Curtis Thanksgiving. Mary Curtis pulled her gray shawl up around her head and hurried back like a hooded bird to the warmth of her house. The powerboat chugged out around the point.

Selina hugged herself into her fur coat as close to the engine as she dared. Thankful hoped when she looked at her that there'd be no motion. Jonathan took an inside course. "Take longer but a dirty sea outside," he grunted. Oh, Lord, thought Thankful, when there on the island was fun and work, and who cared about the weather! Selina was getting paler.

Off the mainland, riding at anchor, long and slim and black as a pirate ship, lay the government cutter. It was, moreover, signaling to them, and Jonathan Curtis attended to signals on the sea. He chugged up alongside.

"Take you up the coast if you like?" Dave, formal, business-like, beside an officer. Selina woke up. "Have to land for supplies this morning. Glad to take you along."

Selina forgot her fear of boats and scrabbled up the

ladder. Jonathan's "Up you go!" was to a different tune. His relief swept Thankful aboard, too, with no regrets. Dave had saved her a bad morning.

The men paid little attention to them once they were aboard. They weren't getting off for an hour, the mate explained, and make yourselves at home. He walked off. Selina gazed after him thoughtfully. Thankful found a sheltered corner and opened a book. When she next saw Selina, the officer was helping her up into the turret where no guests were allowed. Selina had cheered wonderfully. Dave was nowhere in sight.

On schedule the cutter made for open sea. It had none of Jonathan's caution about shortcuts. Thankful's excited eyes watched the swift race for the outer water, a swifter motion than she had ever known. She could hear Selina's squeals of delight. Then the deep lift which Thankful loved, the swing up and the long slide down. Oh, if she could only have gone to sea with Gramp!

Selina's squeals had ceased. Thankful turned her face from the sea to meet her staggering down the deck on Dave's arm. He bent over her pityingly. "Better take her below," he advised. "We'll be only a short time out."

Selina caught at his words. "How long," she whispered, "how long?"

No one even smiled. "Before you know it." Dave made you feel so protected. "Take it easy now, take it easy."

Even for Selina, Thankful could not wish the short

voyage done. She knew how Dave felt about his job. He had sea blood, too. The boat was to him what her island was to her. And if she had been a boy she would have taken the boat, too. She knew that now. But she would be quite content with her own little sailboat once she got back to the island. And now she would understand Dave better when he talked about his job. If he ever did. Well, just let him try talking about it to Selina! Thankful grinned at what would probably happen to him.

The cutter slipped silently up to the big dock and made fast. Selina could furnish only a blue smile for her officer. Yet even on that, he offered to telephone for the school bus. And settled them comfortably in the waiting room until it could come. Thankful shook her head in amazement at the girl!

Selina revived under the jar and shake of the bus which always made Thankful want to walk. Before they reached the school she had forgotten her downfall. Her words, her suitcase, herself, tumbled out at the feet of Robert who was mysteriously at the door when the bus stopped. Thankful listened as she hurried away and thought, If I hadn't been there myself! How she does talk!

And she felt a fierce possessive anger toward Robert who had not cared to hear her account of what really happened. Yet when she was out of the sound of their voices, she could smile at what Robert must think about her home. Thankful felt uncertain about what a manor house was, but she was sure that a cutter wasn't a steam yacht. "And the food!" She caught Selina's ecstatic squeak. Well, no matter what she said about a Curtis Thanksgiving dinner, she could not be too prodigal. But Thankful was jealous for all the beauty of Bright Island which Selina did not know, and which should be hers to share with Robert. Perhaps someday! She instantly submerged such madness but a spark still stayed alive. It made her feel warm and comfortable.

The Business of
Producing Cinderella

Selina considered herself appointed Mistress of the
Wardrobe. Mary Curtis, it seemed, had talked the
matter over with her. Selina now considered Thankful an
heiress and was prepared to clothe her suitably. Thankful
saw a certain amount of danger in the premise but she was

indifferent about the results. She never had been interested in clothes, and her experience here had hardened indifference into dislike. Clothes were the symbol of her humiliation.

But Selina was prepared for resistance. "Don't let her argle-bargle you into putting it off," Mary Curtis had said, and while Selina wasn't quite sure about what it was Thankful might do, she was ready for a prompt attack.

"I've asked permission for us to go to town next Saturday," she announced on Monday.

Thankful looked pleased. "Movies?" she asked. "I've never seen any real ones."

Selina was shocked but other business was more pressing. "Certainly not. We are going to buy you some decent clothes."

The word could always cow Thankful. "What for?" she protested. "I'm used to these now. Maybe I even like them."

"Like them! We leave here on the nine-thirty bus." Selina was finished.

Thankful thought uneasily about ways to escape but none occurred to her. Anyway her mother had given her an envelope full of money and she might as well get rid of it. They left on the 9:30 bus.

It dropped them at the noisy railroad station which Thankful had not forgotten. She admired Selina's assurance in buying tickets. "I've never been on a train before," she said when they had settled into the green plush seat.

169

This time Selina hid her shock. "You sit next to the window then." She spoke as if to a child and they exchanged seats.

Swifter even than the cutter, though without its grace and quiet, past little gray farms, startling grazing cows, stopping now and then with a grating and gritting which hurt Thankful's teeth. She had no word for Selina. She sat, her hands folded in her lap, her eyes following, following. . . . "The movies must be like this," she finally said.

"Like what?" Selina peered out puzzled. But she got no answer.

When her eyes were battered with too much seeing, she shut them, and still the motion went on. It ceased in the darkness of a huge train shed. Thankful followed Selina out of it into a taxi which reared and shuddered through crowds that miraculously stayed alive when it had passed.

"Of course this won't be like shopping in New York." Selina was excusing its size. That at least, thought Thankful, is something I'll never have to do. "But there are good dress shops here and we'll visit them all."

The first one completely satisfied Thankful. "I'll take that one, and that one," but Selina covered her low voice with, "We'll look a little farther. Just give me your card in case we come back." Thankful was sorry for the woman's disappointed face.

The next shop had a dress that surprisingly suited

Selina. To Thankful it was too beautiful! Green blue with a coral belt. Thankful had seen the water at sunset with those colors. She nodded to Selina.

"All right, try it on," Selina consented and the slinky voiced clerk ruffled it over her arm ready for Thankful.

"It's all right anyhow." Thankful was firm.

"You put that dress on before we buy it. Mustn't she?" she appealed to the clerk.

The woman said, "Suttingly," and Thankful pulled off her plaid wool. At least they gave her the protection of a small room which she hadn't expected.

Mirrors, mirrors all around her, and in them she stood abashed, bare arms still golden with tan, pale fluff of hair, startled eyes. The woman ran experienced fingers down her slip. "No girdle?" She lifted eyebrows of astonishment.

"No girdle," said Selina gloomily. She knew this was coming.

Thankful was watching a long pink cube sink stiffly through the water, down, down, to any mermaid that wanted it. "I had one," she said, "but I gave it away."

"Shouldn't have done that." The woman was obviously wedded to girdles. "But of course you aren't the fat kind. We'll try it." She didn't want to lose the sale.

The dress settled over Thankful's shoulders and fell softly down around her. She watched herself in the mirror and bent forward to be sure it was true. Taller, curves new to her, eyes like the dress under their dark brows, hair a blown dandelion. She would like to have Robert see her like this. She turned to Selina who was looking at her with strange woman's eyes, and to the clerk who said, "You need no girdle." She bought the dress.

The success raised her spirits. She was more willing now to go on. Selina was wise in the adult ways of shopping. There must be a woolen dress and this and that. "Sit down," she said, "and count your money." It had dwindled. "Shoes now, and the right stockings," she decided regretfully. Her heiress was falling short. "I'll stand to the lunch," she offered generously. But Thankful paid her share. Though she could have eaten more. All her muscles ached now as they had the day she arrived in weariness and terror. Better a shopping trip than that! she thought with warm recall of the blue green with the coral belt.

At the end she had a coat—she clung loyally to Dave's hat—a dark jersey with scarlet edges, the coral-belted beauty, and shoes whose heels discouraged her. "You'll get used to them," Selina said. "Just practice balancing. You're good in the gym."

"I'll only have to wear them evenings." Thankful, sure-footed as a goat, rocked dizzily in imagination.

Selina made her wear the wool and the coat to save bundles. "They'll mail your old things," she said, and Thankful hoped they would be lost. She liked herself with the silvery fur under her silvery hair.

"Nothing more," she announced. "Finished."

"Sure you haven't any more money? Let's see that envelope." Selina was suspicious. "It's an hour before the train, and there's plenty you need yet."

Thankful opened the envelope. "You don't get that." She removed the last five dollar bill from Selina's grasp. "I've two Christmas presents to buy. Where would I find handkerchiefs, and where would I find a pipe?"

"Ask a floor walker." Selina sat on a bench and shut her eyes. She had spent every cent that she could get, and she was ready to rest.

Thankful wandered about a good deal because she wasn't sure about floor walkers. She found Scotch thistles on handkerchiefs for her mother. The pipe was difficult. She saw nothing that resembled the one her father smoked. Would a little silver filigree be to his taste? She considered and the clerk said, "Take your time," and took on a new customer.

"A carton of cigarettes," he ordered.

Thankful whirled. "Mr. Fletcher!" she cried. "Oh, please tell me which pipe to buy."

The man looked at her with polite unrecognizing eyes. Then the voice seemed to reach him. "Thankful Curtis!" He sounded awestruck. Then, "Have you gone over to smoking pipes?" But he still looked oddly at her.

"Would father like this one?" She held up the silver filigreed pipe.

"Certainly not." That was settled. His long fingers hovered over a severe brown thing. Ugly, Thankful thought. She reassured his hesitation. "Three dollars," and showed him the bills. He dropped the pipe.

The one he decided upon was much worse but Thankful saw no way of getting the silver filigree now. The clerk banded her too large a parcel. Mr. Fletcher rescued it confusedly. "Just a little of my brand of tobacco for him to try. You don't mind?"

He walked beside her with the parcel. "Where now, Cinderella?"

Thankful found herself much pleased with all of her purchases. "Do you like my new clothes? Where do you suppose I left Selina?"

"Yes, I like them, though not as well as the jeans. Do we have to find Selina?"

Astonishing remark. What man hadn't wanted to find Selina? How could he prefer faded overalls? She gave it up. "There she is looking for me. If we lose that four-ten!" She broke into a run.

They raced into Selina's perturbed vision, and Thankful watched again that baffling alteration. Lucky he was with me, she thought. In a minute he and Selina were laughing together.

"What if," he proposed, "we see Greta Garbo and take the next train?"

Oh, could they, could they? But no, of course they were signed up.

"I'll telephone," he said, and met with no opposition.

Selina was terribly excited and rushed Thankful off to the waiting room where she powdered and puffed endlessly. Thankful still felt a stranger to the girl who looked out of the mirror with pleased eyes. Cinderella, he had called her. But he liked the jeans better. She thought of the waves slapping over the boat, and felt the wet hard rope on her hands as they pulled together—we could get old Dinkle some chocolate, she thought, and found that she was including Orin Fletcher. "Ready," called Selina, "we mustn't keep him waiting."

Down the dark aisle with music from nowhere stepping along with them and a strange little creature all legs and arms whirling dizzily on the screen. Then high letters, *Anna Karenina*, and silence. Thankful looked inquiringly at the dark saturnine face beside her, and he nodded. "The same," he said, "but Garbo can do it."

It was odd at first, outsize people talking in enormous tones, familiar words roaring in her ears. Then her eyes began to accept them on their own terms, her ears found overtones, the deep husky voice of Garbo had its way with her. She fought her emotion with island reticence. No one has any right to make me feel this way, she told herself, no one has the right. But Anna at last swept away her sense of herself and she traveled with her through the trackless waste of her suffering. When she ran in terror beside the train peering at the windows, Thankful lifted stricken eyes to the man beside her.

"Don't take it so hard," he comforted her. "It's only a picture."

It was not a picture to Thankful. It was a broken life. She could not bear it. And when at the end that distraught figure came searching for release under the grinding wheels, Thankful felt that she tasted death. She sat shaken, withdrawn. She could move no more than the dead.

Selina bustled for her coat. Under the glare of the lights she looked a little strained. She had hoped for Queen Christina's love affair, and now the best thing to do was to forget it. Thankful made her uncomfortable. She leaned forward. "Come to! It's all over!"

Mr. Fletcher moved between them and held Selina's coat. When he finally had her settled, he turned from her and touched Thankful gently. "It seems bad now but you'll be surprised how soon it will leave you. When you get outdoors," he promised, and Thankful rose.

But it was not gone, even under the lights and life of the city. And in the train shed when the wheels ground to a stop in front of her, she looked at them with such white horror that Orin Fletcher slipped a hand under her arm. She leaned gratefully against him without knowing that he was there.

"The next time it will be Zasu Pitts for us," he said shaken at what he had done to her. She did not hear him, nor would she have known what he meant if she had. But Selina laughed loudly. She only hoped there would be a next time.

The man turned a seat over and faced the girls. He drew the package from his pocket, and as if Thankful were a stricken child, sought to attract her attention. She looked at the little brown pipe, and suddenly the island was real to her again with her father smoking the new tobacco, and her mother examining the thistles. She showed him the handkerchiefs and he admired them. Selina felt out of it. "I shall do my Christmas shopping in Philadelphia," she said and Mr. Fletcher didn't seem to care.

At the door of the school he stood with bared head in the cold. "Think of the brown pipe tonight," he said, "and don't have bad dreams."

Selina was tired and scornful. She had worked hard spending Thankful's money, and she felt empty of reward. "You've certainly got a line," she said. "I wouldn't have thought it of you."

Thankful was too exhausted to care what she meant. She thought about the little brown pipe and fell asleep.

But the sharp purity of that agonized face stayed on with her.

A Stranger on Bright Island

Again Bright Island crept up over the edge of Thankful's horizon. It seemed to her that she counted off the almanac of her year by these uncertain appearances, like a beloved star which you could not depend upon to rise. She read the thermometer and the barometer for long minutes each morning, watching the sky, dreading the cold for the first time in her life. But even if it freezes, she thought, Dave promised to break them out. And after I'm once there the ocean may freeze to the bottom.

It snowed and melted, sleet turned to rain, December was mild enough so far. She knew that her father would come out only through open water, and she walked to the shore to see if the coves were clear. Not even a rim of ice.

The school was electric with the approach of the holidays. Youth milled about in its small enclosed world restless to break away. It poured its energy into the Christmas party which would celebrate the coming of freedom. No one mentioned work and the faculty wearily held only to the letter of it. The place would be emptied out and they were glad of it.

If Thankful could not get out to the island she would have to stay with her brothers on the mainland, and that was a dreary enough prospect. It made the figures on the thermometer more important than those attached to algebra. It made the matter of the holiday dance secondary though she had no dread of it now. The clothes of Selina's choice seemed to carry with them some small share of Selina's confidence. Or it may have been the way the work had gone, or the friendliness of Orin Fletcher, Thankful could not have told herself why she felt comfortable where she had been uneasy. She knew that she would look well enough at the party, and that now she could dance. Of much greater importance was a kindly temperature.

Even with the rhythmic beat of the music in her ears

she gave it a thought. "It's down to thirty-seven tonight," she told Bill who led her off.

"You don't say so," he murmured.

"But salt water freezes late." She looked hopefully up at him.

"Is this chemistry or a dance?" he asked.

"It's a dance," she agreed, and because the bay could not freeze, and Bill liked her and danced well, and she was going home next day, she gave up the weather and attended to him.

Once she had a fleeting glimpse of herself stumbling through the dragging hours of that first party, but it only heightened tonight. Her youth shook off its growing pains and danced with light feet.

No doubts tonight about Robert. He had been lighting her days with that flashing smile of his. He had included her with Selina and then left Selina out. Selina took it philosophically. "He always likes to rush a good-looking girl," she said, "and he thinks he has discovered your looks. He'll drop you if you stay around long enough."

But Thankful knew better. That warm intimate look of his belonged to her. His quick grace, his clipped words, his dark clear face, that were all so new to her island experience with its towering men. He came across to her now, and she slipped like water away from Bill.

"Come out." He was brusque. "Want to tell you something."

She followed to a window seat in the gallery. His dark looks made her tremble a little. "What is it?" she said. "Oh, what is it?"

"Hung up for the holidays," and would say no more until she had coaxed him. There were certain examinations, she found out, if he was to enter his junior year at Harvard in the fall, and they had specially arranged to accommodate him during the holidays. But couldn't he go home first? Chicago did not seem so far away to Thankful now. No, his father insisted on his studying before the exams, and when they were over the holiday was done. He glowered down at the dancers and Thankful longed to touch his smooth dark hair in comfort.

"Where can I stay?" he demanded of her. "Where can I stay? Dad wants me to move straight to Cambridge but what would I do there with everyone off for Christmas? This place is shut up. Where can I stay?"

Thankful felt a quicker beat than the music stir her. Why not? Her mother would welcome him as she had Selina. She might even help him in his study. Her words stuttered and stammered these things to Robert without hope that he would understand. But it was all that she could offer him.

"Do you mean it! Thankful!" He seized her hands, and she thought for one breathtaking moment that he meant to kiss her. "Thankful, you've saved my life again!" The smile flashed back again. "Save it enough times, and it will be yours. Will I come!"

He leaped up and pulled her back among the dancers. Never had she moved so lightly, so surely, as if a warm surge of life caught her and carried her with it. Robert talked of what they would do until she feared the ideas that Selina might have given him, and tried to face him back to reality. But he swept them both on with his charm. Would tomorrow ever come? And could it, whatever its enchantment, make her a more lovely gift than tonight?

By suppertime all the school world knew of their plans. Robert filled her plate and stood looking down on her. "It's as if we were getting engaged, they're so excited," and laughed at the color in her upturned face.

All but Selina. She caught Thankful a moment in the cloakroom and talked gravely to her. "Head this visit off if you can," she said. "You'll both regret it." A little jealousy? But Thankful thought not. Selina's interest in Philadelphia and a West Point boy was too wholehearted just now.

"You did it," Thankful laughed at her, "it was you who told him so much about Bright Island."

"Yes, I did," Selina agreed gloomily and departed.

Only once more she spoke of it. In their room she looked anxiously at Thankful hanging away her dress full of soft tired wrinkles. An odd light was in her face and her lips curved into laughter at nothing. "He's not the boy to hang your hat on," she told Thankful. "Believe me."

For the first time in her life Thankful could not

sleep. She lay flat like a frail figure on a sarcophagus and watched the stars move down the sky. Tomorrow night from her window under the eaves she would see them in their march, a bright battalion in the wider, colder sky. And beyond her in the boys' room he could watch them too—only he would be asleep, she thought, and touched his closed lids with tender fingers. She would see that he rested well, away from all these demands upon him. She made her plans smiling in the dark.

It was a fresh morning full of the gayety of departure when return is certain. Selina said casually, "I can't kiss you because I've just used my lipstick. Almost had forgotten how. Listen, Thankful"—she had an open letter in her hand—"I just heard from Evelyn Norris." Thankful remembered the name with quick hurt through her happiness. "But I don't see much sense in changing roommates this time of the year, do you?"

"No, I don't," said Thankful and the tide of her happiness rose higher around her.

"All right then. We'll let it ride." Selina was businesslike. "I'll tell Miss Haynes. Good-bye. Have a swell time." She was off for the railroad bus.

Since no one traveled their way, the gardener was driving Thankful and Robert in his old Ford. Jed at the last moment had agreed to meet them and Thankful thought contentedly of the size and comfort of his powerboat. The Ford grumbled behind the bus which flung back to them greetings, cheers, advice, farewells, until its high-powered engine left them behind.

"You'd think it was a honeymoon." Robert drew in his head, brilliant with excitement. He turned his attention closely to her. "When I get through Harvard"—his hand shut over hers an instant—"when I'm through Harvard, we'll see!"

The tide of happiness was too high. Thankful choked under its pressure on her heart. She had no answer ready, and in the silence Robert sank back as if deflated. His head pushed spent into the corner, his eyes closed. "The morning after!" he murmured, and Thankful could not bear to rouse him to the first sight of a roughened ocean. He breaks himself up into shiny bits, she thought. Someone should look out for him.

Jed was at the lunch counter finishing a thick cup of steaming coffee. "Better have one," he advised. "Warm you up. Got a cold trip ahead of you."

Thankful drank her bitter cup though she needed no warmth. Robert looked at it with distaste and left it. Jed reached over and drank it. "You'll be sorry, young man." He was jovial. "Well, all aboard!" He loaded an armful of bundles into the shelter of the bow. "Christmas for the kids," he explained. And Thankful looked around startled at Robert because she had nothing for him. He stood beside her on the deck staring at Jed's boat. "Is—is this—the yacht, the boat, that Selina sailed in?"

"She went over to the island in it," Thankful explained carefully. "She came back on the government cutter."

"Oh, I see." He smiled at her and she cheered. "Well, here goes." He backed down the ladder, his raccoon coat brushing the slimy slats. She was suddenly glad of that coat. Though Jed looked at it oddly.

But Robert was too thorough a sailor not to find enjoyment in any kind of boat. Thankful saw him putting away his ideas about a steam yacht and adjusting himself to lesser ones. He was man to man with Jed and before Thankful knew it he had the wheel sitting there in the wind with his collar turned up until she could see only the brilliant dark eyes. "A good coat for this kind of weather," Jed even said, "though a sheepskin does me."

Thankful settled contentedly into the bow. She had not meant to wear her new clothes but Robert's presence demanded high celebration. She pulled her slicker up to protect her fur collar. Jed had looked with approval at her. She grinned to think of the girls.

In spite of the raccoon coat Robert was shivering before they were halfway to the island. Thankful beckoned him down to the shelter beside her. He gave the wheel promptly to Jed who said, "Bet you wish that coffee was in you instead of me now," and opened the top button of his sheepskin.

Thankful peered up over the rail now and then to point out the light, Goose Island, Egg Rock, but

Robert ducked back out of the wind so quickly that she gave up sightseeing. The smell of the engine was heavy in her nostrils, and she knew that with the old coat she would be outside at the wheel with Jed. She reached up her head to catch the cold wind in her face. Robert was here beside her incredibly sailing out to Bright Island.

Even through the noise of the engine Thankful heard the crash of the tide on the bar, and knew exactly how high it was, and how near the cove, and when she could see gleam of the white boulders, and then the house. Here, and here, and here, yet she sat without moving in the shelter of the deck, Bright Island submerged by Robert. He was cold and uncomfortable but they would soon have him in the warm kitchen. Kitchen? He wasn't used to kitchens. Ah, but this one, sunned and spicy, anyone would like this kitchen. Hadn't Selina? Jed was waving and she plunged to her feet.

Though Robert stood beside her, she forgot him for one moment. The house, low-roofed and bare against the frozen slope of the island which lay behind it brown in a December cold that had as yet brought no snow, her father shoving his peapod down the beach, her mother's face between the curtains, all there, all waiting for her.

"Whose house is that?" Robert was there again. "I thought you had the whole island to yourself."

"Why, it's our house, of course," Thankful laughed at

him. "Whose else would it be?"

Robert said nothing while Thankful caught the mooring with the boat hook. Her father was almost out to them when he stood up in his peapod and stretched to see them better. He took to his oars again with a grunt and pulled alongside. Then he rose again staring at Robert.

"I thought to God you had a b'ar aboard!" he said astounded. Jed's roars sounded as if they had been long held back.

Robert looked over at him coldly, and Thankful saw him with those critical eyes, woolen cap tied over his ears, long, lanky, brown, grizzled. "Bar, did you say? Your son is too good a sailor to run on the bar." The silky reassurance of the words stung Thankful. Jed's roars abruptly ceased. Jonathan said huh uncomfortably, and sat down to wait for them to come aboard.

The encounter seemed to rouse Robert to his old elation. He swung his leather suitcase into the peapod and followed it with an armful of bundles from the shelter of the deck. Jonathan took them automatically without looking at Robert.

"Hey, there!" shouted Jed. "The kids' Christmas presents! Put 'em back!"

Thankful got into the peapod and handed the parcels back to Robert who took them with an intimate flashing smile at her that drew her to him against the other two. Thankful tried to include her father by a belated clumsy introduction which he ignored. Off on the wrong foot! she thought despairingly.

But Robert had just got into his stride. When Mary Curtis met them at the door he delivered himself into her hands with such courtesy and charm that she took him to her heart at once. Another boy, and she was used to boys, who was cold and probably hungry, and undeniably handsome. A bonny lad if she had ever seen one. Not too strong either, her shrewd eye told her. And it took less than a day for her to check up on her surmise. She knew then exactly when Robert had been laid low by infantile paralysis and the kind of childhood that grew out of it. She knew why he was spoiled, and how, what he needed, and was careful that Thankful learned nothing of it. "He's a right to outgrow it," she said to Jonathan who had to be told in order to make him live in the house with Robert.

"If he can!" Jonathan grunted. "He'll get no help from me."

But now she put an extra plate on the table and lighted the Franklin stove in his room before she would let him go to it. The winter fare had set in. Mary Curtis fed her family bountifully but the island had to furnish supplies. She thriftily put the meat which Jed had brought into the cellar way, and served the dinner already cooked for Thankful. Creamed codfish and baked potatoes with Thankful's favorite Indian pudding. Thankful ate it hungrily until she saw Robert's plate. Her mother met her puzzled look and rose to pour him another glass of the top of the milk.

Robert, who had given up rising when she stood, thanked her and thirstily drank the milk.

"I'm never hungry for lunch," he apologized, "but I'll make it up at dinner."

Thankful could not swallow. Could they, she thought desperately, shift to dinner at night? And knew that they could not. But Mary Curtis had set a jar of golden apple jelly beside his plate and he was spreading his bread richly with it.

"I'll warm this up for you then," she said. "We have our hearty meal at noon."

Robert did not seem to mind at all, and Thankful knew that her mother would always see that he had enough. So that hurdle was over. But Jed did not bother to say good-bye to him, and her father went out with his son and did not return until dark. There were other hurdles, Thankful saw.

Robert slept all the afternoon in a room glowing warm with the wood fire which Mary Curtis tiptoed in to replenish when it burned low. She and Thankful talked in low tones downstairs about him, and the dance last night, and Thankful gave her many facts empty of substance. That lovely evening. And to be talking it over in this sunny room with its familiar chairs and table and worn couch where she had lived before she ever knew Robert; it made her feel confused as if she were two persons and the one did not know the other. The confusion slipped over into drowsiness from the sleepless night, she leaned back against the old cushions, and her sentences came slower and slower.

Mary Curtis tucked her gray shawl around Thankful and stood looking a moment at the sleeping face, defenseless, innocent. Then she shook down the kitchen fire for a hot oven for her biscuits.

When Thankful woke, the room was so dark that the firelight made golden squares in the open damper of the stove. She watched it warm the colors of the old rugs on the painted floor, and thought drowsily of trees massive enough to furnish those wide boards. She heard her mother stirring about in the kitchen and knew from the smell of hot biscuits what she had been doing. For Robert—she plunged out of sleepiness, Robert was here! And suddenly the peace and security dropped away leaving her shivering with responsibility. What if he had spent a bored afternoon in his room while she slept? She threw off the shawl and hurried to the kitchen.

"Well, you had a sleep!" Her mother was setting the table for supper in the kitchen as usual. "And the lad's still at it. Better call him. He won't sleep a wink tonight."

Thankful hesitated. She had often banged on Dave's door and even pulled his hair when he refused to stir. She thought of Robert lying asleep with those long black lashes on his cheek. "You go, mother, while I finish setting the table."

Her mother was gone a long time and came down smiling absently. She put a small piece of beef on the toaster to broil. "He'll be down in a minute. Robbie's a bit peevish when he first wakes up," and she chuckled.

Robbie! Thankful knew now that as far as her mother was concerned, the island was Robert's. Well anyway, she thought, he can't have Robbie's plaid because that's mine. But she was not at all sure but what she, herself, would have handed it over to him if he had wanted it. She sighed at her folly and brooded over its sweetness. When he came into the room it was as if a new lamp had been lighted. She saw him through its radiance.

Robert sniffed greedily. "Steak!" He took a look at it. "Please! It's done, it's done. Oh, please take it off! I like it rare."

Mary Curtis removed it to a hot plate. "Well, Robbie, you've got to eat it, but it looks raw to me."

Jonathan came in from the darkness and washed his hands at the sink. He sniffed, too. "You been hacking up that roast?" He peered at the plate. Thankful died a thousand deaths.

"Yes, I have." Her mother patted a piece of butter into it serenely. "Want some?"

Jonathan answered only by helping himself to a hot biscuit. Robert shot him a triumphant gleam. He cast off the final remnant of after-sleep temper and cut vigorously into his steak. His gayety rose like a thermometer under the heat of discord. He likes it, Thankful thought uncomfortably, but could not believe herself.

The hot meal and his sleep seemed to pour energy into Robert. He was as restless as quicksilver while Thankful and her mother did the dishes. Mary Curtis handed him a dish towel but he held it helplessly and finally dropped it in a tour of the room.

"Looking for something?" she asked.

"I thought if you didn't mind"—he smiled winningly at her—"I'd start the radio. Then maybe after you are through, we could dance."

"We haven't a radio," Thankful announced shortly. He knew that, he knew that it took electricity to run a radio.

But she misjudged him. He apologized and explained in detail about the kind that ran on its own batteries. "I'll send you one." His face lighted with zeal. "I'll send you one as soon as I get back."

Thankful warmed at his generosity, and her mother smiled tolerantly. "I'd like it fine," she said. But meantime there was no radio.

Thankful thought that she had never known so long an evening. Jonathan, sunk behind his newspapers fresh from the mainland, emerged at nine, lighted his lamp, and stalked up to bed. With his departure Robert's sparkle unaccountably died down. When Mary Curtis followed with, "Better get to bed. The day's left you well ramfeezl'd," he remained standing, a little lost.

Thankful watched him drearily. Never once aware of her, she thought. Showing off to irritate her father and charm her mother. And now bored with no audience. He turned back to her and her heart melted at his smile.

"Come over here." He motioned her over to the old sofa. "Now perhaps we can have a little time to ourselves."

So he had thought about her, he had wanted to talk to her. It was only his courtesy to older people which had made him ignore her. The room glowed again into warmth and life.

But Robert was tired of talking. He tried to pull her head down to his shoulder which was uncomfortably low. "Now let's have a little necking party," he suggested in a business-like tone. He kissed her hard.

Thankful's head plunged upward knocking his teeth into his lip. In an instant they were facing each other in a fury like a pair of fighting cocks. Thankful calmed first. "Let's not," she said, and wanted to laugh at his fallen crest, and to cry at something that hurt her.

"Oh, all right." His anger petered out. "But what fun *can* you have here? Anyone would think you'd never kissed a boy except your brothers," he added in light scorn.

"Well, I don't know as I have." Thankful considered it honestly. "Except, of course, Dave." She thought of Dave with a rush of friendliness.

"Who's Dave?" Robert was sharp.

"Dave? Why, Dave's Dave. You know sort of in the

family." She was vague in her confusion. "You'll see him Christmas."

"If I'm here," said Robert darkly.

Thankful turned startled at the foot of the stairs. "Why are you going, Robert?" She must not let it sound like the heartbroken wail it was.

"I didn't say I was." The storm was over and Robert's smile flashed again. "Not till after Christmas."

She climbed the stairs wondering, because now that it vanished she discovered that a faint relief had been there. Not until she opened her window and looked out at an island under a cold half moon did she realize that she had given it no greeting and the day was gone. She sighed.

The stars marched high and wide as she had expected, but she sighed again because she knew that Robert was not looking at them. She rubbed her lips, and buried her face away from the sky. She was conscious of the faint resonance of the sea, everywhere, as if the very walls of the house were vibrant with it. Part of the rhythm of her breathing. Would it, she was anxious again, would it keep Robert awake?

The Stranger Leaves
Bright Island

Unaccountable, that sense of relief, but it was there again fleetingly when Mary Curtis established Robert and his books at her kitchen table after breakfast. He resisted, but only halfheartedly after one look at the weather. He had come downstairs blue with cold though Mary Curtis had early lighted a fire in his stove. He had hovered over the kitchen stove, turning and turning, yet still he shivered. Thankful watched him, regretting for him the suffocating steam pipes. She was cold, too, for she had no fire in her room and missed the warm kitchen where she always dressed in the winter. I'm getting soft, she thought, and shivered too, though more for Robert than herself.

She buttoned up her sheepskin and pulled a dark knitted cap down over her cloudy hair. "Wind's gone round northa'd," she observed, "and the barometer's dropping. May get snow."

She was not prepared for the effect of her weather report. Robert crashed back from the table to the window. "Snow! Snow!" He sounded doomed. "What'll we *do*!"

Mary Curtis turned from the stove, hand on hip. "Do about what?" She smiled tolerantly at Thankful's disturbed face.

"About getting away, about getting back, about being stuck here—well, you know what I mean." He broke off apologetically. "I'm due for those exams so soon."

"Now don't fash yourself about that," she reassured him, "snow makes no drifts on water. And the storm, if there is one"—she looked warningly at Thankful—"has days enough to make and break before you go."

Robert rubbed a finger on the frosted window. "Of course," he said, "I have to allow some time to get to Cambridge. Perhaps I ought to leave before Christmas."

Thankful sat down suddenly. She unbuttoned her coat feeling a little sick. Even those three days until Christmas he could not stand. Over there by the window, alien, remote, as if they were jailers holding him on the island. She could feel him searching for some way to escape. She would help him.

"I could run him over to the mainland." She looked carefully at her heavy boots. "And then"—she thought her way along—"he could stay overnight at Pete's. And there's that early local to Smithtown. And I think a bus there which ought to connect with something . . ."

"Tut, tut, my lass!" Mary Curtis broke into the itinerary. "What tillie-vallie! You and Robbie are a pair! Just hunting for trouble. What if it does snow a whiff or two? Did you never see snow before? We'll get you there for those examinations, my lad. And now you'd do well to set yourself to the business of getting ready for them. Out with you, my girl, we're at work."

Thankful stumbled to her feet. As she closed the door she heard the amazing sound of Robert's lighthearted laughter. "I wouldn't trust my precious neck in that little motorboat with her anyway. . . ."

"You couldn't have a better pilot," her mother said soberly. "We'll start with the Latin."

At first the day seemed unalterably spoiled. She toiled up the path, stopping at the little graveyard to brush the dead leaves from Gramp's stone. She had a sudden vision of him with Robert and put the vision away as suddenly. But the thought of Gramp stayed with her and little by little edged away the image of Robert. Her barometer rose in spite of weather. Here was the island, free and open, when it might have been piled high with drifts. And would be yet, she thought with a grin, if she knew what those ragged spitting clouds meant. She couldn't begin now, after all these island years, to worry about the weather. They'd get Robert back somehow. And let it blow and drift and freeze them in solid after he was gone! The spring would be soon enough for her to get out.

She put away one of the sweet secret plans which she had made lying wakeful after the dance. By afternoon Christmas greens might be covered with snow. She ignored the surmise that Robert would be unlikely to leave the warm room. Mary Curtis always liked the house hung with ground pine and fragrant with the pungent moss which grew at the far end of the island. Thankful would see that she had it. Though a shadowy boy which should have been Robert moved all the way by her side.

Down through the crooked paths of the empty sheep pasture, toward the end of the island where the great white rocks piled their beacon. The wind stung her face and she knew that it must have veered a point to the east. The crash of surf would have told her anyway. She crouched in the shelter of a boulder and saw indigo dark water all around the island, creamy-crested here, sending fine mist of spray into her face. It was freezing on the smooth boulder, and soon she felt that it was freezing on her. She stamped her feet and ran down into a sheltered hollow where the moss grew soft and thick, all its pungency chilled out of it.

The moss filled her arms so that the ground pine had to trail around her neck. She covered herself well with it, for by now the light gusts of flakes had begun. She found scarlet branches of black alder, and small hidden partridge berries and wintergreen, and bound them into bundles with ropes of ground pine. As she gathered them, cold, rich with color and fragrance, she became a part of each bright berry, each green streamer. She was as much the island as they were.

She burst into the kitchen frosted with snow, hung with green and scarlet. Her arms were numb with their cold burden and she covered the kitchen table with it just as Robert swooped it clear of books and papers. With her entered a great gust of snow-freshened air, which Mary Curtis breathed deeply. Robert leaped back to the stove and stood there, hands behind him in its warmth, smiling at her.

"She's a pretty gal, isn't she?" he said confidentially to her mother.

Mary Curtis was mopping up the dust of snow. "Better help your father haul up his peapod before you take your things off. Full tide tonight."

Robert sprang into action. "I'll help him. Wait till I get my coat."

But Thankful could not wait. He was gone too long. She could hear the scraping of keel on pebbles. The boat rested well above high water mark when Robert crashed down to them.

"B'ar cub!" muttered Jonathan.

"Like to see my boat before she's snowed in?" Thankful wanted to offer him something.

Their steps made a dark line of prints through the powder of snow over to the sheltered end of the cove where the *Gramp* was hauled up. Already the island was stirring as if the tumult at the far end had disturbed it. Snow gusts blew in their faces, stung their eyes.

"What in heaven's name is all that hullabaloo?" Robert shook his head as if to rid his ears of a roar in them. "Went on all night. Isn't it ever quiet here?"

Thankful was conscious then of sound. The air, the earth, the sea, were filled with it, like herself, and as unaware of it as she was. A great tuning fork, it set them all to singing together.

"Nor'easter," she explained briefly. "You won't hear it when the wind shifts."

"Will it be a bad storm?" Robert was really anxious.

"Tell better when the tide turns. Just a smurr, I guess."

The neat curves of the hull of her boat on its cradle rose shoulder high before them. Thankful laid a greeting hand on its stanch keel. Robert walked around it with critical eyes.

"She's a good boat," he said warmly. "I bet she can make time."

Thankful gleamed at him under snow-misted lashes. "I'd like to try her against your boat." He must not see her pride.

But there was none of the sailor's quick rise to her bait. Robert looked gloomy. "I'm not so crazy about sailing as I was," he muttered.

Thankful was shocked. "Robert! Your beautiful boat! You wouldn't give her up just because she capsized!"

"Well, isn't that enough!" He was growing impatient.

"Handle her right and she wouldn't." Thankful was pleading for a friend. "She's not as seaworthy as this one, but all she needed was a reefing."

Robert laughed her off. "Tell you what," he said. "Next spring if I launch her, you shall sail her."

Thankful thought of spring days with Robert's boat, bacon over driftwood fires, Robert lounging comfortably with her at the helm, and her heart grew so warm and bright that a sudden slash of snow across her face seemed from another zone. "I'd be glad to," she said, and realized a faint sense of disloyalty to the *Gramp*. She moved her mittened hand down the lovely curve of its bow, tested the snugness of the canvas cover, pounded a slat with a beach stone, before she left the boat alone in the gathering storm.

She thought, I wish he wanted to see the surf on the cliff, and knew that he wouldn't. She followed his hasty retreat back to the warm house. Mary Curtis had broiled a finnan haddie, and its pungent smoke met them at the door. Would Robert eat it? He sniffed appreciatively. "I'm hungry as a—a bear," and Thankful knew that he had started to say b'ar. But he asked for a second helping of the flaky buttered fish, and ate enough gingerbread to satisfy even Mary Curtis.

The afternoon dragged. Robert dozed on the couch over a required volume of Milton. Now and then he moved uneasily to the window with, "Will it be a bad storm? Is it getting worse?" Each time Jonathan, feet on the oven shelf, grunted from the kitchen. The smell of his wet boots seemed to annoy Robert. Mary Curtis darned stockings in her rocker by the window and looked upon the storm as if she liked it. Thankful moved, restless, from the one room to the other, missing the concord which had somehow cemented them into one.

"Get the corn popper," her mother finally said to her. "The fire is just right."

Robert dropped his Milton, and scorched his face over the popcorn. The corn, too, Jonathan grumbled, pushing it around for white kernels. Small pointed drifts rose up the edges of the window sashes. The island deepened its note outside, answering the storm. The kind of day which Thankful loved. What was the matter with it today? Without Robert, she thought, and would have no more to do with the idea.

The dark came early, a kind of white dark filled with misty arrows of snow. Jonathan creaked out to his chores. Thankful seized her coat from the nail, filled with the energy of the long tight day. "Be back soon," she called, and caught up the wooden snow shovel which Gramp had made her years ago.

Outside, the deep rumble of the sea seemed to shake the very snow. It twisted up as well as down and drove in crazy patterns past the yellow squares of window light. Thankful dashed into it with long vigorous strokes, following the dark prints of her father's boots which led to his bobbing lantern at the barn. He would not bother with a path until morning when he would know the storm's capacity, but she could not wait.

Down, up, and over. Down, up, and over. Her body caught the rhythm and delivered it, down, up, and over, to her mind. The restlessness passed. Again she was part of the island, wrestling with it against the storm.

When her father came back down her small dark lane with his steady pail of milk, she felt his pleasure in her. She knew vaguely that it was not the path, but something that she had left behind her there in the house. She fell into line behind him, her shovel over her shoulder.

"Be over before morning," he said. "Wind's already comin' round," and she listened with him to the storm's change in key. She felt toward her father a quiet gratitude as if he had saved them from a disaster.

She stepped up closer. "Think the good weather will hold then till after Christmas?" and strained to hear.

Jonathan held the door with his foot for her. "Might," he said, "or might not." But she thought he meant that it would. It must. What if they could not get Robert off the island! But they could. Dave would. She comforted herself with Dave.

Again Robert woke up in the evening, and persuaded Thankful to dance while he whistled, sweet and shrill, in her ear. But the floor gritted, and she stumbled under the sardonic eye of her father, and Robert grew impatient and gave it up. Thankful went off drearily to bed, taking care to leave while her mother was still talking to Robert. She had shoveled paths and so she slept, but her dreams were disturbed.

A west wind blew the morning in. Thankful looked out at their own bay, feather white with crisscross waves. Under a ragged blue sky it was turning indigo and green. The deep boom of the outer rote had softened into a murmur that Thankful would not have noticed if she had not been listening with Robert's ears. Bright Island gleamed so white that her eyes could not open wide to its splendor. But a glimpse of her path showed her that little more snow had fallen. Only today and tomorrow, she thought, and shivered into her clothes.

With the sun, Robert's spirits rose. Mary Curtis could hardly hold him to his morning's stent. He had asked, "Will the wind go down?" and when Thankful nodded, had seemed to free himself of all threat of imprisonment. It was, perhaps, the pleasantest day of his visit. He liked the sweet-smelling Christmas greens, and put some of his own grace into their order. Thankful thought that the old rooms had never been so lovely. He even persuaded Jonathan to cut a small tree, and hung it zestfully with corn which he managed to keep unscorched, and cranberries which he found in the cellar. He kept busy and happy all through the day which finished up the storm and blew fair weather for their Christmas.

The sun rose so late that Thankful thought it would never creep up over the edge of the island. Then she remembered that the shortest day of the year was over, that now minutes of light would add to their days and shorten their nights, that the year was rolling around to where it would stop in its orbit and release her from the weary round of counting off its days. Short days or long days, they were all filled to the brim on Bright Island. Spring was not exactly in the offing, she thought. Steel cold sky and sea, shifting and darkening into still colder blue, a glittering island rising white and frozen out of it, no yellow warmth in the sun. But the shortest day was over! Though that would be small comfort to Robert, she thought.

Mary Curtis made the day ready for her sons and their wives. "They'll be here just long enough to eat," she said practically, "and we must not keep them waiting. It's luck indeed"—a swift glance out of the window as she cleared the breakfast table—"to draw such a quiet day out of the winter."

Robert stood by the window. "Looks pretty rough to me. And cold. Isn't it colder?"

"Aye, a few degrees, and still dropping. But don't fash yourself, Robbie. Salt water freezes slow."

Robert looked relieved. "Which one is Pete?" he asked idly, and listened to her brief biographies of her sons. She liked to talk to him and this morning there was no time for lessons. Though Robert said there was no need. "It's no wonder you know so much," he told Thankful. "She makes you learn." His quick light mind had broken restlessly away from her steady penetration. His books were all packed.

Thankful for the first time in her life had plunged into an agony of preparation for a family dinner. She had dreaded it for Robert so deeply that she forgot her own dislike of it. But Robert, his recurring weather problem settled, seemed to have high hopes for the day. Nor would he allow the tree which he had installed to be neglected.

The Curtis family had perforce made little of gifts at Christmas. A few small hand-fashioned gifts when they had a shoal of children about, often now a quiet day with only Thankful left of them all. The question of a gift for Robert had troubled Thankful until she forgot to enjoy the thought of the pipe and thistled handkerchiefs, her first bought presents. But her mother had brought out sheepswool slippers, fashioned and sewed for her. "They'll fit Robbie," she said. "He's small." Thankful had flinched at small, and she wanted the slippers herself. Somehow one didn't seem to have unmixed emotions in connection with Robert.

But when he put them on and leaped like a tawny-footed faun around the room, with flying blue ends of a knitted scarf meant for her, her eyes stung with shy delight in him. Her father took his pipe and left the room, a stiff embarrassed back. Her mother laughed at him, and tucked her handkerchief in her belt where the thistles would show. Robert had hung a large white card in place of the angel, he said, an elaborate promissory note for the delivery of a radio. "He acts as pleased," Jonathan muttered, "as if he'd given us one."

The island had to furnish its own Christmas dinner, and it came out of Mary Curtis's plentiful cellar. Chickens could not be spared for roasting when their eggs would be all too scanty for the long winter. But months ago she had provisioned against this need. She brought up tall mason jars filled with the tender meat of the August brood, and a jar with peas, small and green behind the glass. Thankful found the whitest onions in the bin, and the smoothest potatoes. She uncovered turnips and carrots, and wished for a turkey such as Selina had shared. But there would be plum pudding with burning brandy as her mother knew it in Scotland. And the girls always brought over a box of candy for Christmas. Those girls! She could hear Robert's light mocking laughter of them, and felt down there in the cellar rooting about in the vegetable bin a sudden strong loyalty for her own people. The girls might annoy her, but let Robert beware!

But Robert approached them with nothing but admiration for them in his dark eyes. Thankful marveled again at him. He anticipated their every need, and she could see their significant glances at the boys. Husbands never endowed them with such grace. Robert made these great island men ponderous and ill at ease. But the women fluttered and fussed even more than they had for Selina. Yet they still had an eye for Thankful's bright wool and knew well that they had not bought it for her. She enjoyed that! But the rest was too anxious, too strange. She, herself, hardly knew Robert in this guise.

She felt the aura of his charm move outward to include Pete. The other men he ignored completely, but Pete he treated as another man of the world. And Pete, dapper in his store clothes, preened himself. He was, Thankful noticed, nearer Robert's size.

"Jed's bringing up a box that was left at my store for you," Pete told Thankful. Jed staggered up the path, and Pete flung the door wide. "Want it opened up?" And while he and Robert looked on, the other boys opened the big wooden box.

Out of the excelsior they drew a small gleaming radio with Selina's card attached. "This is for your mother but you may listen to it." Mary Curtis was pleased and put the card in her apron pocket. Thankful ached for Robert. His lovely idea taken from him. She had no place even for Selina's generosity.

"Well," said Robert lightly, "she got ahead of me, didn't she?" and he removed the white angel card from the tree.

"Let's see," said Ethel, and they all oohed and aahed at his disappointment. Only Jonathan still looked skeptical.

With the mail was a letter from Selina which Thankful took into the kitchen to read to her mother. The boys with Robert directing were setting up the radio. Selina was business-like as usual.

> I thought your mother might enjoy listening
> to a radio when it got too cold to go out much.
> I got Robert to help me select it because he
> has one on his boat. Hope it works all right.
>
> Love, Selina

She had read the sentence about Robert before she saw its implication. She stared at her mother, astounded. Mary Curtis continued to pour the gravy out in a smooth brown stream. When she spoke her voice was gentle.

"Dinna fash yoursel', my lass. Robbie meant well. He gets so used to his own fine words." She chuckled. "But it was terribly handless of him not to reckon on Selina."

Thankful's eyes blazed under the dark wings of her brows. Within her was an intolerable hurt. She had only young hard judgment for Robert. He was little and mean and full of devious ways which she could not meet. Her scorn was a devouring flame which burned away her sorrow. She started for the door, the letter stiff in her outstretched hand.

Her mother blocked her way, gravy bowl balanced against a dish of cranberry jelly. "I wouldn't do that, Thankful," she said.

"He mustn't pride himself that he can do this to me." Thankful was stubborn in her pain.

"It will hurt you none. And he hasn't so much to pride himself on. He's not going to pass those examinations."

Thankful looked piteously at her mother and gave her the letter which went into the pocket with Selina's card.

"Now it's as if nothing had happened. He's your guest." Mary Curtis was suddenly stern. Thankful snapped out of the self-pity which clogged her throat. She took the dishes from her mother and carried them with unsteady hands to the table. Robert was in his element explaining the mechanism of the shining instrument. Ethel exclaimed in admiration at his knowledge, and Thankful shut her teeth over, "Why wouldn't you know?" He was her guest.

"Dave's coming over if he can make it," Ethel announced. "The cutter'll bring him in. He telephoned from down East last night. Had a little icebreaking to do first."

Thankful's beaten spirit stirred. Dave was honest and strong. Nothing could keep on aching so hopelessly if Dave was around. If she could see him sitting there at the table where they had often shuffled off family dinners together, if she could see his honest blue eyes and sun-bleached hair she might forget for a moment that dark flashing smile which hid dark thoughts that made you ache. Wanting to see him so much, she started for the window and met Robert's eyes, shrewd and thoughtful. She could not look at him, but he did not seem to notice.

"Will the cutter come after him?" he asked casually.

"Sure," said Ethel. "He's got in good there, I tell you. His father told me he's pretty certain of promotion at the end of his year."

Dave getting promoted! That was as it should be, Thankful thought, and she felt family pride swell her sad heart. Dave coming today, with the immediate help which he always managed to give her. The day seemed caught out of its artificial chaos into natural order. She and Dave could always manage. She wondered fleetingly how he would get along with Robert, and knew that none of these fine manners would win him. And if Robert chose, he could make almost anyone uncomfortable.

But Robert seemed to be watching as anxiously for Dave as she was, and when the slim cutter hove to outside the cove and dropped its dinghy, he looked unaccountably relieved. Dave was rowing himself in, and hauling the dinghy up the beach. That meant the cutter would be back for him later. Mary Curtis set an extra plate and began to dish up the dinner.

Dave crunched up through the snow and into the crowded room, reaching for Thankful while he bent over to hug her mother. Thankful smelled the cold sweet air in his uniform, and feeling him tower over her thought that he must have grown. But perhaps it was because she was used to Robert. . . . She turned quickly to introduce him. And turning, felt Dave's arm stiffen on her shoulder. She looked up at him, startled, and he dropped his arm, bowing abruptly.

"Didn't know you had company," he said.

Robert laughed, a little artificially. "I'm not company," he said, "I'm one of the family."

Thankful believed that he meant to please her. But for once she knew exactly how her father was feeling. He and Dave, standing so tall and glowering, a welcoming pair indeed! And perhaps she looked the same way. She rushed into the kitchen and seized a platter of chicken. Robert was equal to them.

212

Thankful sat between Dave and Robert and felt herself a receiving station for them both. Dave's antagonism bristled through her to Robert who curiously enough deflected it with ingratiating questions about Dave's work. And Dave could not resist an interest in the cutter. Thankful felt his fierceness abate and was filled with pride at the effect of his intelligent answers until she caught Robert looking attentively out of the window. Even through her resentment she marveled again at him.

"Getting pretty cold for you, isn't it?" Robert played with his plum pudding. The dinner was nearly over.

"Cold? This is nothing. You should see us under steam when it really is cold!" Dave accepted another helping.

"Nothing I'd like better." Robert was cordial, excited. "I say, you couldn't take me aboard this afternoon, could you? You did mention that you were calling at the port anyway, didn't you? You could drop me there easily. Say, that would be swell!" He leaned forward to look at Dave, his eyes full of the dark fire that had so moved Thankful.

Dave took an unnecessarily large mouthful and was a long time quiet with it. Thankful waited without moving. Oh, if he only would take Robert away! Yet she could not bear to see this stratagem succeed. Where Robert was, no feelings were simple.

Dave laid down his fork. "Too bad," he said, "but this isn't a passenger boat."

Thankful looked around at him imploringly but he

still stared at his plate. Robert was not discouraged. "I will, of course, pay well," he offered.

Thankful could see Dave's forefinger tap the edge of his plate. It was a strong brown finger and it managed somehow to look implacable. Dave's voice was still gentle, but in it a latent tone which Thankful recognized. Robert would do well to go slowly. Though she suddenly found that she no longer felt responsible for Robert's comfort. He could take too good care of it himself.

"I don't know as you or anybody else has got money enough to buy a ride on that cutter."

Robert always knew when he was beaten. "Sorry," he said stiffly. "I understood you took the girls over in it without any trouble."

"No, there wasn't a mite of trouble," agreed Dave pleasantly. "They went on a special invitation. Well, I guess I'd best be going. I hear 'em tooting for me."

He would not let the family leave dessert, and said good-bye to them all together. But when his tall blue shoulders went past the window, he turned his head and catching Thankful's eye he winked. And suddenly laughter flowed over the sore pride and healed it. Dave had never failed her yet!

Robert had plunged into a feverish line of conversation with Pete about his store. Pete was being important and Thankful knew what would happen to him. She could not bear to wait to hear it. She rose to bring fresh coffee.

When she came back it was settled.

"Your brother has kindly invited me to spend the night at his place," Robert said deprecatingly. "I think perhaps I'd better accept so that I can get off before it freezes. He says we're likely to have it colder."

Thankful nodded, angry at the final stab of pain. She filled the cups and went back to the kitchen with the coffee pot. Robert's overshoes were drying under the stove. She would take them up to his room so that he would not forget them when he packed. At his door she stood still. The room was bare and clean of everything which belonged to Robert. His bags stood packed and closed ready to go. Had she thought that stab of pain was final? She set the overshoes carefully together on the leather suitcase and closed the door of his room, so that her mother would not see.

Back in the dining room there was already the stir of departure. Only Ethel sat still, a glazed look over her face as if she had turned inward thoughts on bedding for the spare room, and how much Pete had in the way of canned goods to eke out. She came out of her trance to cast a horror-struck look at him when he jocularly abetted Robert in his urge that Thankful come along too.

"We'll have a swell time traveling around the world to get back to school. We'll make them open up for us. And I'll come right back after the exams. Come on, Thankful. Be a sport. It'll be an awful bore to go alone. And anyway you'll get frozen in here."

Thankful thought of what a day on the train with Robert would have meant, what long days together in the deserted school should mean, and wondered because now there was no meaning.

"Nothing would make me leave Bright Island," she said fiercely, "and I hope it will freeze solid to the mainland."

But Robert only laughed at her. "Bet you'll regret it," he said.

"I bet she won't," spoke up Jonathan unexpectedly, and Thankful was grateful to him.

"Better be moving." Jed was herding his passengers. "Get your things packed, young feller. Got to get back before gas freezes."

Robert looked alarmed. "It won't take me long to pack."

Thankful thought, no, I guess it won't. Then to her mother who was going to help him, "Why don't we wrap up the bricks on the back of the stove for them?" and rushed to the kitchen.

Robert was back reasonably soon. "How about me for speed?" His head emerged from the great fur collar brilliant with excitement.

Jonathan muttered, "B'ar cub," but shook his hand limply. Mary Curtis patted his shoulder warmly, but she was too honest to wish him success with his examinations. She looked touched when he turned back at the door soberly and kissed her. Then like quicksilver he tried to grab Thankful but she dodged him. They parted with laughter.

Jonathan offered to row out a load in his peapod, and Mary Curtis shut the door against the icy afternoon. Thankful started to speak to her about the cold, but her throat thickened so that the words would not come. Her face began to work, she made a mighty effort, gave it up, and rushed upstairs to her room.

Her mother wrapped up the last warm brick, and got a sheep's wool comforter from the cedar chest. She opened Thankful's door softly, and with competent hands covered her until only the cloudy head buried in the pillows was visible. Then she left her in the quiet room with the sound of Jed's motor going across the water, fainter and fainter. It was Mary Curtis's belief that a lass must do her growing alone.

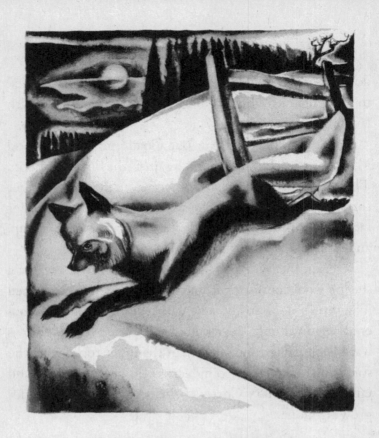

Breaking Through Winter

When Thankful woke next morning she felt as if she had been out in a storm which had left her battered but had washed her clean. She turned on her side to watch the sun ride up into the clear dawn. So she had watched it since she was a child, and so she would watch it, she knew, as long as her eyes could see. Robert was but a small incident in her island-ordered life. She heard the stove lids thump, and smelled the bacon and coffee. This was home as it always was, and she vaguely hoped always would be. She felt herself once more one of its native elements, merging into it. Robert had lighted like a dragonfly and gone as fleetingly. Down deep something yearned over the beauty of his flight. But the glory of the dawn, and the homely sounds beneath, made everything else irrelevant.

Thankful sprang for her clothes. A new and vigorous current flowed through old channels and rushed her back into island life. She seemed to herself just arrived in her eagerness to get her hand in again. She was dressed by the kitchen lire and pouring out the oatmeal when Jonathan wheezed in from his chores.

"Cold," he said, and he looked pleased to see her there. "Cold, and getting colder. Nor'west wind come up with the sun. No kind of weather for b'ar cubs." He stopped short at a warning look from his wife. Then as if to make amends, "Feel like helping to haul out a mite of wood this morning? We're shy of cord wood and I got a piece cut over."

It was like haying again, only in the bitter, bitter cold. They harnessed old Sparrow, reluctant in any temperature, and followed his bumping sledge down the wood road to the clearing. The snow was so thin that in the shelter of the spruces they had to help push over gritty places. Sparrow expected it and waited for them to ease his load. "Pull as hard as we push and you'll get some-where," Jonathan grumbled.

But he acted as if he liked having Thankful there. The two strode along in companionable silence, collars up, ear lappets tied down, pants tucked in heavy boots. The thick woods were a windbreak but the urgent cold was numbing even through thick mittens. Thankful would be glad to get her hands to work.

At the clearing they blanketed Sparrow who stood in a coma while they loaded the sledge. "Can't take much at a time," Jonathan said regretfully. "Snow's too thin." Thankful bent, lifted, and piled, feeling the return of her old strength and knack. Wouldn't do to stay too long away, she thought. I'm going to be stiff tomorrow.

But today was today, and its work warmed her and filled her with tingling satisfaction. The wood smelled clean and dry, and a red fox ran across the clearing, and the clouds sailed high in wind that bent the treetops and turned her face scarlet. They trudged back and forth three times, stopping once to thaw out at the kitchen stove. When the shed was stacked along one wall with wood for drying and splitting, Mary Curtis called them to dinner.

Thankful peeled away the layers of coats and sweaters impatient at any delay. The platter of fishballs, crisp brown with creamy insides, dwindled and emptied. She divided the last one with her father who said, "Et more today than all the rest of the time you been here."

"She always liked fishballs," Mary Curtis said.

Thankful wanted to go back to the clearing in the afternoon but "Nuff's enough," Jonathan said. "If I got my work all done today there'd be nothing left for the rest of the winter." So Thankful curled up on the couch to read a little, and talk a little, and to look out of the window at a hard bright day which made the old house creak, and finally to doze a little until the day grew steel dark.

Her mother called her from the shed. "Come out here, Thankful. You've a caller wants to see you."

For one stifling half-awake moment Thankful thought that it was Robert, returned to torment her. She staggered to the door strewing her books, catching the gray shawl about her head. It was Limpy! He stood there by the door balanced on one leg, reproachful. His great white body was sleek in the cold twilight, his wings its color. He looked at her and flapped them.

Thankful took the pan which her mother held out to her and caught a coat from the peg. "Has he been here every night?"

Her mother nodded reluctantly. "Aye, he's a lazy bird."

Thankful walked out toward Limpy who lifted heavy wings but changed his mind when she shook the scraps. "Small wonder he doesn't know me," she said bitterly, "when I'd forgotten him."

But her mother was back in the kitchen.

Limpy ate the scraps in gulps while Thankful shivered over him. When he had finished he rose with a long screak and sailed into the dark. Thankful's eyes followed him. "You'll eat out of my hand tomorrow night," she said. "But I wouldn't force you tonight." She shivered again. It was bitter cold. And Robert had nearly taken away so much from her!

The oven door was open and inside its warm cavern Thankful could see the brown pot of beans, its crackle waiting to be skimmed. Her mother was cutting across the round loaf of steaming brown bread with heavy string so that it would not crumble. The kitchen had the Saturday night fragrance which had so haunted Thankful at school. She stood contentedly by the stove waiting for her father's step. Then she reached into the oven with padded fingers and pulled out the sweet-smelling beans. They filled the deep dish with the pork, transparent and rich, on top. She ate slowly and long with a deep savoring of home.

Thankful slipped back into the rhythm of the days as if she had never been away. Except for a sharpened awareness in her senses. She found herself taking nothing for granted, the snugness of the house against the gnawing cold, the threat of the booming waves, the clean thin air, even the winter fog which shut them in with a dank gray blanket colder than snow. She realized them sharply now and put them away for dull days to come.

It grew steadily colder during the week, and Thankful watched the ice gather, crunch in the tide, pile up, and finally fill in the cove with its rough blocks. Jonathan had hauled up his powerboat, and Thankful felt as if a lifted drawbridge cut her safely off from the land. No mention was made of the day after New Year's when she was due at school.

No more snow fell, and the island lay under a thin icy crust. Each morning until the wood shed was filled, Thankful and her father creaked through it to the clearing. The steady work hardened her. Her muscles stopped aching and so did her heart. She seldom thought of Robert, so little was he associated with Bright Island. He had gone as lightly as the dragonfly and left as slight impression. Except that even yet she could not bear to hear the radio. Her father sat over it by the hour, and her mother hummed its tunes. Selina would be pleased.

"Bring down the books I lent Robert," her mother said. She had not called him Robbie since he left. "We could have a try at Harvard ourselves."

Thankful went into the cold empty room which might never have held Robert, and brought down the pile of her mother's books. They sat over them enjoyably and though Thankful grew sleepy sometimes from her hours in the winter wind, she got back some of her old zest in them.

Over higher mathematics Mary Curtis balked. "Too niffy-naffy for me," she said. "I cannot abide them. But elsewhere I'm still in the lead." And would be, Thankful thought ruefully, for a long time.

"Would you like to go on to college, my girl?" Her mother leaned her floury hands on the table and eyed Thankful keenly. "I understand from Robert that only two years would be needed there."

Thankful stopped scowling over a problem to look at her mother with amazement. "I wouldn't if I could," she said, "and anyway I couldn't."

"Might," said her mother looking relieved. "Might as far as money goes."

"If I had a million," said Thankful, "I wouldn't waste it that way. And I spent all you gave me on clothes. You ought to see them!"

"Like to," but Mary Curtis did not go back to her work. "There's something I'm minded to tell you now that the yammer and yawl is over."

Thankful rested her chin in her cupped hands and lifted puzzled eyes. "What about?" she asked.

"The island. Bright Island." Her mother wasted no words. "Your Gramp left it to you. It is ours as long as we live, of course, but then yours."

Thankful's fingers made white dents in her cheeks. "Mine?" she whispered. "Mine?"

"Yours, and your children's," her mother affirmed. "His will read *To my granddaughter, Thankful, the only true islander of the Curtis brood.* He's right, too. But that didn't hinder the boys from getting bleezy over it. They wanted to sell it to a yacht club. Aye, we had great doings that you knew naught of. But they're over it now." Mary Curtis straightened as if a burden were gone. "Though the girls will be blethering about it the rest of their lives. But they keep it under cover, and there's no ill will toward you, my lass."

Thankful still stared at her mother under dark brows. Bright Island was hers, hers to stay on as long as she lived, and for her children after she had left it. She need never live with the girls on the mainland if—sometimes in dark hours this dread clutched at her—if she were left alone. The island belonged to her just as she belonged to the island, always and inseparable. She felt her own youth and its age in her together and found the confusion hard to bear.

Mary Curtis helped her. "Say naught of this to your father. He takes it hard, too, that the boys were cut out. Though he'd take it harder if they sold the island." She chuckled. "It's a man's world, Thankful, and they like to think they lead us. You would never be a good follower. Your Gramp knew it." She handed her the colander. "Now pick me out some sizable potatoes for baking."

In the dank cold cellar, Thankful picked out, discarded, chose automatically. She did not know that she was chilled until her mother opened the door and told her to hurry. The horizon of her life had widened so suddenly that she was dazzled. She could not see its edge. She washed the potatoes at the sink and heard her mother say, "And so when you think it over, if you want to go on with your learning you could sell off a piece and manage fine."

Sell off a piece! Would she cut off her own hand and sell it? The confusion quieted into clarity and exactness at this one problem. For more years like this last, she had no desire. A dulling of what had been sharp and enjoyable, a tearing down of what the island had built up in her, an obscuring of her own values. She felt these things vaguely but surely. "I have thought," she said. "I belong here."

Her mother nodded, and whether she agreed or not Thankful never knew. But she did know that her mother had given it to her to make her own decision, and she was grateful. She had enough to do now with all this glory on her hands. School bore but a small part of it.

On New Year's Day Mary Curtis baked a large chocolate cake. When it came out of the oven, its fragrance drew Thankful to the kitchen.

"The end piece?" she begged, hanging over it.

"No," her mother said, "not a crumb. It's for Selina."

Thankful looked aghast. "Then you might as well give me the end slice. For I'll not be getting back to Selina until it's stale."

"That's as it may be," Mary Curtis said. "But you get none of this cake unless Selina gives it to you."

Thankful moved uneasily to the window. The thermometer outside said zero, the bay bore out its reckoning. Ice out to the streak of open channel. Thick enough to last the winter through, too, unless an unexpected thaw set in, and Thankful saw no signs. What could let the drawbridge down now? Unless Dave . . . but that promise lightly made meant nothing. For years the island had been marooned by ice with no interference from outside.

Yet even as Thankful watched, the narrow dark shape of the cutter churned up the channel. "You knew"—she swerved on her mother—"you knew they would come. Oh, I don't want to go! I don't want to go!"

"It's no matter what you want," her mother told her. "You'll finish what you've begun. Now stop skirling like a gull and get your things together. They'll be an hour getting in."

"But why," wailed Thankful, "why, when they have never come before do they have to bother us now?"

"No bother at all," said her mother briskly. "We'll like it brawly getting papers and mail now and then. It's a new rule for the islands. Don't stand there looking doited."

Thankful bestirred herself. And suddenly as she pulled off her island clothes she felt excitement pour through her like new wine. She dressed by the window that she might not miss the cutter's advance. It was edging about to point its sharp nose at their old pier which reached farthest out into the cove. Dave was out there, Dave who had promised to get her out no matter how thick the ice. For once she wished that you couldn't depend upon Dave to keep his word. And yet there was that high excitement rushing her on to be ready for him. And a little crowing like a young rooster because she could go that way and Robert couldn't!

She had brought almost nothing with her, knowing that the island could furnish her with everything she needed there. She was ready in her coat and hat long before the cutter had sliced its way to the end of the pier. Her father had heard it and left his wood chopping to come in and watch where it was warm. They stood together at the window and Thankful felt some of her own excitement in his tense body.

"God's sake, look at 'em climb!" he muttered.

The scooped bow slid up over the ice and crashed down through it by its own weight. Patiently it backed out of its crevice, mounted the ice bank, and crushed it into a jagged aisle through which it edged its way. Slow, persistent power, lowering a new drawbridge over which she must pass. She could feel the thrust of her own muscles when the cutter drove itself through the ice. A good name for it, she thought.

Mary Curtis put a glass of milk and a fresh cookie into her hand. "Better have a snack even if it is early," she advised. "Who knows when you'll eat?"

"Or what?" said Thankful mournfully. She crunched the buttery raisin-sweet cookie as if the school fed her on bread and water.

Her mother reached for an empty coffee can. "Too bad about you. I meant to give all these to Dave, but I might save a few for you."

Thankful observed the can. "Look at the size of Dave's box. Four times as big as mine!"

"Aye, and who's giving you a ride?" A piece of twine made the box safe.

"Who wants a ride?" sighed Thankful and set the glass of milk down.

"Finish that milk," commanded her mother. "You know well you'll like it fine pounding through that ice."

Thankful felt an ecstatic leap of desire to be out there in the fierce cold, grinding implacably down the ice channel to the swift rush through free water. The weight on her heart at leaving her island, hers as never before, was eased by the way she was leaving it. Dave had helped her out again.

"He was a good egg." She tried this on her mother. "I won't crab about the cookies."

Mary Curtis chuckled. "You mix your figures a bit, my lass. That's the school. Well, here you are. We'd best be leaving."

They loaded up and started for the old pier. Thankful felt the winter cold gnaw through her smart coat as it never had under the old sheepskin. But she had no regrets. Dave had been proud to take Selina aboard.

She trod the rotten boards of the unused pier with

sure feet and stood waiting to be pulled aboard at the last rush of steel bow. Dave leaped past her with a bundle of papers and mail, hugged her mother, and rushed back with all her odd bundles.

"Up with you!" A hand from the men leaning over the rail, a shove from Dave, and she was up the short rope ladder.

"Watch that cake," her mother called.

"Who's it for?" shouted Dave.

"Selina!" cried Thankful.

Dave swung the box dangerously over open water.

Thankful grabbed it. "You've a batch of cookies that would fill a wood box," she said.

Dave crowed, patted his stomach, and waved thanks to the two figures on the beach who had already turned back against the biting wind. Their bent heads pushing against it touched Thankful through her excitement. She knew well that within an hour they would both be busy about their own concerns, but somehow for a flash they seemed to need her youth between them, canting forward with them.

"Nice hat you've got," said Dave in her ear, and never mentioned the coat. But she liked the glances of the other men though Dave assured her that they were attentive only because they so seldom saw a girl on board. Perhaps, she thought, and was glad that she had worn her good coat. She felt oddly different from the girl who had sat by herself on the deck while Selina captivated the officer. More grown up, surer of herself. She had a vague sense that after all Robert had made her a gift, even if it lacked a printed label. But she was not ready to be grateful to him.

Dave mentioned him only once. "Heard your friend spent the whole day getting back and threatened to sue the railroad because he nigh onto froze to death."

Thankful tried to look sorry, but she saw him too clearly huddled in his fur coat, scolding the conductors and brakemen. She had too sharp a memory of Dave's wink as he marched by the window after his tiff with Robert. No, she would never worry about Robert again. But Dave should not have the satisfaction of knowing it!

At noon she had dinner in the cabin with the officers. Dave sat at the end of the table but the steward placed Thankful next to the captain. A big blowsy man who mumbled his words into his beard or his food so that she could understand only now and then. But there was hot roast pork, and boiled onions, and enormous potatoes. They do themselves well, small wonder Dave's so big, Thankful thought, and found that her glass of milk had not even turned the edge of her hunger. Over the rice pudding the men warmed into digs at each other which brought gruff laughter. Thankful laughed too. She was used to a tableful of men.

Just as they finished, and it was a rapid meal heartily eaten, Captain Gilkie spoke straight at her. "Dave's a smart sailor," he said. "He'd go far if shipping wasn't dead. A few more years and this bay'll forget what a keel looks like."

Thankful felt the bitterness of his words and tried to probe into them. Did he mean that Dave's work was hopeless in its future? Dave, who was due to have a promotion? Who knew the sea and how to master it as she knew her island? She looked up into his massive face, bewildered.

The wrinkles creased about his eyes. "Look like your grampa, b'God. There was a man that knuckled under to none. Got out just in time, though, if he meant to keep it up." The gloom came back. "No place on the sea for an able man these days." He shoved back his chair and they all rose. "But we'll keep an eye on young Dave. You better, too. He's a good feller to hang on to!" He chuckled and went off lighting his pipe.

The cutter was already moored to the dock when they came out of the cabin. A few men scurried around, pinched and blue with the cold. Broken ice slashed unceasingly against the piles of the wharf, but already it seemed less cold to Thankful. Less cold and less clean with the musty dampness of the old dock. She felt again the deep urge to go back instead of away, and knew that she would always feel it when she had to leave her island. It would be too long now before she would see it. She looked mournfully up at Dave and saw that he was loaded with her bundles ready to go ashore.

"Rest of the day off," he explained. "Mind if I take you back to school? Nothing else to do," he added hastily.

"Oh, Dave! Then I could show you the school and everything. Wait till I telephone for the school bus." Thankful tossed her sadness overboard, and started for a telephone booth.

"Hold on! School bus nothing!" Dave was lordly. "We'll spend no time waiting." He hailed a taxi.

"You'll spend a good deal of something else," Thankful prophesied, but she liked the idea.

They dashed off through the traffic and Thankful was pleased to note that Dave sat on the edge of the seat. He held the box of chocolate cake on his knees.

"Selina may not be back yet," Thankful offered.

Dave paid no attention. His worried blue eyes were following the cars which whisked by. When they turned into the road by the sea he relaxed his stiff shoulders.

"That so?" he said, and Thankful had forgotten what he meant. "Well, I wouldn't mind so long's I got another good look at the lad with the fur coat."

Thankful ignored him. She wondered herself how she would feel when she saw the lad with the fur coat. Back there in school she would have no defenses against his charm. That background where he reigned might, from its very power to magnify him, draw her back as one of his subjects. And she did not want to be subject to that kind of person.

"I'm here," said Dave.

"Why so you are!" Thankful thought how queer it was that with Dave you never had to be wary about anybody's dominance. They just went along together. She began to feel a little reassured about this first meeting with Robert. If only Dave would behave himself, she thought, half hoping he wouldn't.

But she need not have worried. Dave held the taxi while he took Thankful's things into the hall. Selina's feet flew over the stairs so fast that they scarcely touched until Dave's iron arm fended her off. He looked a little alarmed, but pleased at the warmth of her greeting. In the confusion of arrivals he towered immovable, his blue eyes missing nothing. Selina admired him openly. Robert was nowhere in the crowd milling about the wide hall.

Dave presented the chocolate cake to Selina, almost, Thankful thought with some resentment, as if he had made it himself. And Selina seemed to feel the same way about it. But in spite of her urging he would not stay. Better not, Thankful thought, with that taxi ticking away at the door! He shook hands formally with them both and edged his way out leaving his officer's cap on the table. Thankful ran after him with it and found him mopping his forehead while the taxi driver tried to persuade him to go back for his hat.

His face crinkled into a wide grin when he saw it coming and he jammed it onto his head. "B'gosh, Thankful," he said, "I never had any idea what a sport you were!" The door flew open and he caught a glimpse of Selina still on the run. "Beat it!" he cried to the driver and the car slewed off down the drive before Selina had reached the bottom step.

She hooked her arm in Thankful's, wholly undaunted. "In a hurry, wasn't he?" and forgot all about him. "Say, Evelyn's back, and is she mad at me! Oh, don't mind," she said to Thankful's disturbed face, "Robert is comforting her. Now, buck up, my gal, I might as well tell you before someone else does, she's Robert's new girl!" She halted before opening the door to see the effect on Thankful.

"That so?" said Thankful. "Let's get inside. I'm cold." And to her enormous relief she found that cold was practically the only feeling which disturbed her.

Selina sighed because she had no broken heart on her hands and carefully balancing her cake box, led the way upstairs. In their room she cut them each a large square and delivered the news. Robert had heard by the morning mail that he had failed pretty thoroughly, and now he was in a mood. Selina said that nothing but his pride was hurt because he didn't want to go to Harvard anyway. Evelyn's father was a movie producer and she was going to see about getting him into the movies. "And that settled me," Selina said mournfully. "She always promised to put me in if I'd be her roommate."

"Why didn't you then?" Thankful finished her cake

and took off her hat, twirling it thoughtfully on one finger.

"Well," Selina did have an engaging grin, "I like the one I've got."

Thankful had a quick vision of herself that first night at school last fall, and felt warm and pleased. "Robert would be good in the movies," was all she said.

A Course in Navigation

The winter moved slowly on. Protected from its force, remote from its progress, Thankful could no longer realize it as time passing. The weeks seemed to her like waves at sea, each one like the other, rolling up and flattening out, leaving no record behind. Her island almanac did not read true for these steam-heated rooms and indoor sports. She felt that she had no way to check up the march of the seasons and that winter might mark time forever.

When the midyear examinations at the end of January stirred up a flurry of excitement, part pleasure at a break in the monotony, part real terror, the contagion of feeling caught Thankful. She studied harder than she needed and enjoyed looking at her wan face. She shared Selina's expectations of failure though secretly the examinations seemed so easy that she thought their menace must lie in some fiendish system of marking. She finished up the semester with great ease, as did Selina, and mailed the record of her achievement home to her mother, still a little puzzled at its high quality. Mary Curtis mentioned it in her next letter as casually as if it had been an extra good box of blueberries. Thankful forgot the examinations in the agitation of choosing new courses.

She wavered between following Selina into art or electing a course in philosophy, wanting neither. Robert settled the matter for her.

"Too bad you girls have to take such dull stuff." It sometimes seemed to Thankful that he took unnecessary pains to impress her. "They're offering a course in navigation for a few of us seniors. Only the fellows interested in boats," he added.

"Guess I'll take it," said Thankful unexpectedly.

Robert looked shocked. So did Selina. "You couldn't," he said. "It's not meant for girls." But he watched her uneasily.

Thankful considered. A course in navigation was, she felt, exactly what she needed. With it she could meet Dave on his own grounds. With it, and this thought she would have shared with no one, she could realize a little of Gramp's life even while she followed his orders here. She had a conference with the head of the mathematics department and elected the course in navigation, the only girl. Robert pretended not to see her there.

At the second meeting Orin Fletcher strolled in and seated himself at the seminar table with the small group of students. "Permission from the Dean." He grinned at the instructor and shoved a blue slip at him. "I've always wanted to know the laws of navigation."

He wasn't very good at it either, Thankful thought, when it came to working out the problems. He never knew the proper logarithms. She helped him all that she could but she felt that he took her diagrams rather lightly. She told him one day that he could use the right equations if he would put his mind to it, and then was horrified at her impatience when she remembered how his Latin had set her on her school feet.

He agreed. "You'd be surprised at what my mind's on," he said. Then when she looked at him suspiciously, "Bought me a car. Secondhand, low grade moron of a car, but can she go!" He grinned boyishly at her.

After the car was delivered and somewhat repaired, he offered Thankful rides in return for a certain amount of tutoring in navigation. "I expect we'll find occasion to apply all we know to this car," he remarked to its dark interior when they were stuck in the early mud of a shore road. Thankful enjoyed their explorations and even learned to drive irregularly on a straight pavement. But she found it difficult to secure the proper attention for navigation problems. "I've enough of my own," he said.

Selina became openly envious of the perquisites of the navigation course. "If I'd known Mr. Fletcher was coming into it, nothing would have kept me out," she mourned. "Here I sit drawing little pictures of geraniums while you go joyriding all over the country! And who knows what else will come of it!"

"What else has already come," remarked Thankful. "The class goes on a field trip Saturday, guess where?"

Selina tore a geranium in two. "Wherever it is, I'm going."

"Not you," said Thankful, "we're going to study navigation firsthand on the government cutter. President Davis arranged the trip."

"My officer's cutter? Dave's cutter? The one I rode on?"

"That very steam yacht. And at last Robert's going to get aboard her," and Thankful marveled that it made so little difference to her.

"It's practically settled then." Selina's tone convinced both herself and Thankful. "I'll see Prexie during office hours."

On Saturday, a brisk March day, Selina accompanied the group of navigation students to the government cutter. Thankful never knew how she managed it, but she suspected that it had something to do with herself. She could almost hear Selina offering a companion for the only girl with all those men. And she was glad to have her along. The officer, Dave, Orin Fletcher, where would Selina's laws of navigation take her this time?

Selina, very trim and as nautical as the March wind allowed, settled that problem at once. Captain Gilkie had commissioned Dave to conduct the party and Selina stuck to his side. Her questions dealt less with navigation than with him, and Thankful thought that he seemed to answer them with more pleasure than the technical ones of the instructor. After a deep, curious look at her and Orin Fletcher standing together, he paid no further attention to Thankful. She watched him, proud of his great size and quiet ways. Proud at the way he turned aside Robert's heckling. She had told Orin Fletcher warmly about him and she felt a little hurt at Dave's indifference.

But the day through all its bluster smelled of a spring that Thankful knew would not come to the wind-driven coast for weeks. Still the water had changed from its winter indigo and steel to a fair blue, and Thankful read the island signs in it. Spring would come now, she knew, and even as she watched, winter seemed to step from marking time into a quick march past her. No one could really hurt her on a day so filled with promise. She lifted her eyes from the outer water, feather white in the wind, just as Dave's speculative gaze slipped away from her. Orin was watching her, too, and she felt uncomfortable, stripped of her thoughts until he smiled at her.

"Navigation problem one," he said. "How long would it take at plenty of knots an hour to whip across to a certain island so many miles out at sea?"

Thankful laughed. "It's no wonder," she said, "that you have a hard time to get answers to your problems. You have to be exact in navigation." But she bent her attention upon the shining instruments.

They were not unfamiliar to her. Gramp had found her, of all the children, a willing listener. Together they had charted their course across many a mapped ocean. In his neat shop she had learned respect for the polished tools which could guide a great ship to safety or to destruction. She would have made a good skipper, Gramp said regretfully, and Thankful cherished his praise.

Now she listened absently, hearing his voice through the Captain's explanations to the boys, answering a question put suddenly to her as if it had been Gramp. Captain Gilkie was getting interested in his own talk.

"We'll put out to sea a bit," he decided. "It's no more than a school lesson unless you see her under way."

Selina looked uneasily at the rough outer water and then toward the land. But Captain Gilkie was already in the pilothouse and his orders sounded final. She jiggled Thankful's elbow. "You don't suppose anybody'd have a piece of gum, do you?"

Thankful shook her head. "Just sit still and don't talk. You'll be all right."

"No, I've got to keep my mind off it," Selina muttered.

Thankful watched her anxiously for a few moments keeping her mind off the boat's motion with a feverish zeal which drove Dave into retirement. Then she forgot her, lurching down to the lower deck with the boys to watch the change of course. The water rushed past their very feet smashing its spray over the slippery deck. Its roar and speed rushed her senses along with it until she was part of it again.

The cutter swung suddenly to port and met the waves full on just as Selina, with no further hope of keeping her mind off them, dashed toward the low rail. Her feet slipped on the wet deck. She swung against the swift turn of the boat straight into the roaring water.

Out of the clamor a bell clanged, the cutter slowed, men's feet rushed back and forth, life preservers leaped frantically into the waves, and Thankful was stripping off her heavy coat, all, all in one moment of frenzied time. Not a chance, she knew, that icy water, the heavy clothes, seasick and dizzy, what if Selina *could* swim! Selina, she must get Selina! A great figure wrenching off its coat as it ran, shoved her back, balanced an instant, and plunged like a plummet so close that she felt the rush past her. Dave! It was Dave! Headed straight for that small white face with the red gash of a painted mouth. He would get her! Dave could get her!

Dave had her easily, slung across his shoulder, not trying to swim toward the hastily lowered boats, treading water, easing the gagging gasping head. That bitter, bitter cold water! And Selina so soft, so unhardened to anything. Thankful shrugged impatiently back into her own warm coat that someone was forcing upon her. Orin Fletcher kept his arm across her shoulders and she felt it tremble.

"She's all right, she's all right." He shook her gently. "Now come with me and we'll fix something hot and dry. She'll need it." Thankful hurried gratefully after him. Dave would need it, too.

In a small empty stateroom they gathered blankets and hot water bags and steaming toddy which the Captain, upset and angry, brought to them. Then Selina staggered in, held between two stout sailors who passed her over to Thankful with infinite relief. Selina looked with bleary satisfaction at the worried men crowding out of the door.

She drank the toddy and revived instantly under the heat. "Getting shipwrecked seems to be my line," she said shakily. "And not such a bad one either."

Thankful rasped a harsh towel over Selina's tender

skin. She was filled with the fury which follows panic.
"Try that once more," she slashed with an even rougher
towel, "and I'll swim out and hold your head under."

"If you'd been holding my head instead of Fletcher's
hand, I wouldn't 'a' drowned. And quit skinning me!"

Thankful gave up. You'd have to do more than rub her
skin off to change Selina. And anyway she was here. She
gave her a mighty hug.

Dressed in the cabin boy's clothes Selina tried to push
a wave back into her hair. "I feel fine now the boat's standing still," she observed and Thankful realized that they
must have docked. "Look kind of cute, don't I?" But her
lips, washed pale of their rouge, suddenly trembled and she
turned away from Thankful. "Let's go home," she said.

But her clothes had to be dried in the engine room and
the captain, still gruff, insisted upon lunch for the girls
and Orin Fletcher, who had stayed behind the rest to take
them back to school. A gloomy enough meal with Dave
in overalls glum at the end of the table, and the captain
wholly resistant to Selina's wiles and intent only on emptying his boat of inconvenient passengers. Selina made
one arch attempt to treat Dave as her hero and promptly
gave it up. But she ate a good lunch and thanked the captain prettily for it.

Outside, Thankful started for the engine room when
above the hatchway she saw Dave's tousled head peering
around. He looked relieved when he found her and beckoned.

"Hey," he whispered loudly, "my pants are shrinking. What'll I do, Thankful?"

"Your beautiful blue suit?"

He nodded gloomily. "I'll look like a bluebottle fly by the time it's dry. What'll I do, Thankful? It's up to my ankles already."

Thankful sat on the edge of the hatchway. "Might tie flatirons to the legs." It seemed natural to be devising ways and means with Dave.

"Got none. And anyway that'd make 'em too tight. That empty-headed little hell-diver! Why can't she stay on land where she belongs? Why can't she?"

"Well, I guess she will now," encouraged Thankful. "But it's too bad about those pants."

"Too bad! You got no idea how too bad it is! Thankful"—out of the gloom his eyes lightened—"I'm to see a man about a job that'll set me on my feet for life. Wait till I tell you about it. So many darned people around I couldn't get near you before . . ." Dave swung himself up beside her and they sat in the lee of the wind while he told her.

The high March sky unfurled its wind clouds above them, and the wind hummed through the rigging, blowing excitement through them, drumming them into the future, their thoughts the sweet fifes. Dave's words stumbled but his eyes were steady, on Thankful. She listened, the sunshine golden in her upturned face.

Dave was to try for pilot of a great steamship, the one which was landed high and dry on an island by a city pilot last summer. No Maine pilot had ever grounded a ship. A man had to know the course and currents and the winds as he knew himself. A stranger was bound to be caught by one of them. The company had applied to the government cutter for a good man, and Captain Gilkie had recommended Dave.

Here Dave's excitement quieted. "I hate to leave the cutter," he said, "but the Cap says we'll be aground ourselves soon. The planes do all our work in the winter now. That's why they let us break out the little islands. And if I'm to have no winter work, he says take a big job that'll pay enough for the year. Winters I could"—he gave Thankful a quick speculative glance—"well, I could do most anything I wanted to."

Thankful's eyes dreamed warmly over his plans. "There's the island," she said. "You could always come back there."

Dave stood, his great bulk towering beside her, and up among the humming winds she heard his voice, "I could come back only one way. . . ."

"Thankful! Thankful!" Orin Fletcher doubled his lean body around a lifeboat, tried to withdraw when he saw them, and stood like a bent tree under the boat. "Sorry," he said, "didn't mean to interrupt. The cutter's getting under way." He backed out.

"Thankful," Dave whispered hoarsely, "what about my pants? How'll I go to New York with 'em up to my knees?"

"Borrow some." Thankful shook out of her high mood.

"Cap's the only man as big as I am," groaned Dave.

"Borrow his." Thankful was brazen.

Dave slid down the hatchway. "I bet he's got some old ones I could press. He never throws away anything! Say, don't tell that girl," he called back, "she'll have me swimming all over New York harbor!"

The drive back was quiet except for Selina who, squeezed between them among the gears, chattered about her swim and wrapped rugs around herself until no one could move. Her ruined clothes concerned her little.

"Time we went shopping again," she said. "You can't wear that winter coat all summer. Remember, Mr. Fletcher? You helped Thankful buy a pipe last time we went."

"Yes, I remember."

Thankful did not even hear them.

Selina veered to another tack. "What I'd like to know is what Robert did when I went overboard. What did he do, Thankful?"

What did he do? Thankful tried to remember him. "I don't seem to know. Maybe he threw you a life preserver," she suggested.

"I bet he did. I bet he threw the one that nearly hit me in the head." Selina was spiteful. "I bet he did."

"He yelled," said Mr. Fletcher helpfully, "he yelled *Help* till some of the boys muzzled him."

Selina tried to shrug her shoulders but gave it up.

The car turned from the shore road and chugged up grade. In the clear twilight Thankful could see that curved beach where old Dinkle housed his boat. The days are longer, she thought, much longer. The sky is bright like spring. He'll get his boat off, and we'll have Saturdays for lobstering, and soon it will be time to go back to Bright Island. And she fell to dreaming of Bright Island, and her own sailboat slipping through the blue water, and winter, winter with perhaps Dave there. But only one way, he said. And she thought about that awhile but came to no end with it. . . .

The gears ground them to a halt before the door. Inside, the wide hall milled about with young people filling the hungry wait for dinner with excited talk. The boys had spread the news about Selina and the girls poured upon her with terror and rapture. Selina was at home again, in her native element. Captain Gilkie had somehow put a damper upon her glory. She tore herself away reluctantly and was dressed and back again before Thankful was out of her bath.

It was Saturday night and Selina danced indefatigably. As she danced, the story grew. Thankful could hear snatches of it passing her, drowsy in an armchair. She had been in bed an hour when Selina woke her with the snap of the light. By now she had learned to defend herself from it, and she rolled to the dark wall. But Selina would have none of it.

"Wake up." She sat down hard on the bed. "Wake up while I tell you."

Thankful held a moment to a Bright Island dream, it escaped her, and she blinked up at Selina.

"Evelyn's in such a stew that she made the nurse give her a sleeping powder. Said she couldn't sleep a wink all night thinking about it."

Thankful tried to follow her. "Must be she's really fond of you."

Selina snorted. "I'll never keep Evelyn awake. The matter with her is that she just can't bear it because Robert so nearly lost his life trying to save me!"

Thankful sat up in bed. "Yelling?" she asked. "Or heaving the life preserver at your head?"

The girls doubled up.

"He's good." Selina stopped laughing to admire. "He's better than I am. And I'm not bad at stretching a story, now am I? Funny thing, too"—she looked puzzled—"not one of those boys gave him away. And neither did I."

And neither did I tell about his Christmas radio, Thankful thought.

"You know Robert's going to get somewhere before he's through. I shouldn't wonder if he got to be the president." Selina yawned and Thankful yawned.

PART IV

Back to Bright Island

Scudding Before Heavy Weather

Mary Curtis was dying. Unbelievably dying. The telegram in her hand said those words to Thankful but they were not to be believed. Her mother could not die. She liked life too much to leave it. She was too strong and busy to die. There was some mistake. The boy couldn't have meant the telegram for her. She turned it over. Thankful Curtis. That was her name.

The messenger on his bicycle had called it out to her.

"Where'll I find her?" he shouted. "School's closed for Easter, ain't it?"

"I'm here," she said in a small foreboding voice. "I'm Thankful Curtis."

The boy had tossed her the yellow envelope. "Saves me riding up to the office," and wheeled away.

She stood under the lilac bush, a moment ago sweet with its tight buds, a moment ago startling with the robin's first song, and forgot that spring had ever stirred her. It said—it said—what did it say about come at once? Oh, yes, she must come at once. Her mother was dying.

She tried to move, staggered a little. I'll have to sit down a moment, she thought, I feel queer. She bent her dizzy head on her knees. A car chugged to a stop beside her.

"Wake up, Thankful! I've got the lunch. Old Dinkle's not going to wait for you to take a nap." She lifted her head. "Why, Thankful, *what's* the matter?" Orin was out of the car. "What *is* the matter?"

He took the telegram from her limp fingers and read it. "My poor darling," he murmured. Then very business-like, "Get into the car." He moved a huge basket for her and she knew vaguely that it held their lunch. Then she was back at school and Miss Haynes was helping her to get ready. She was conscious of relief that Selina was not underfoot. And that she, herself, had refused the house party.

"I should have gone home anyway," she said dully. "I should have gone anyway."

"Of course you shouldn't!" Miss Haynes packed briskly. "If she had flu your father was quite right to tell you to stay here. One's enough to have on his hands. He couldn't know it was going to turn into pneumonia, could he?"

"I should have gone anyway," Thankful repeated. She may have needed me. I could have helped, she thought. She would want to see me before she—but she *couldn't* die! You had to be sick to die and she was strong. You couldn't get pneumonia on the island, you couldn't. "How do you suppose I'll get back?" she asked.

"Thank the Lord Mr. Fletcher was around." Miss Haynes handed her her bag. "He's down at the door waiting. He'll get you over somehow. Your poor father was probably too distracted to make any arrangements."

Thankful hardly knew that Miss Haynes kissed her gently or that she was talking in low tones to Orin Fletcher. She huddled into the seat and stared at the dusty hood. Should have cleaned it for him, she thought.

As they tore over the crest of the shore road they saw old man Dinkle's boat putting around the point. Out into an incredibly blue bay where people rode the waves happily, and hauled the lobsters, and laughed because spring was here. She could almost see herself, splashed, gripping the wet slats, pulling, pulling—yet this was herself, her only load the weight of grief upon her. How could you be two such different people in so short a time!

"I've done some telephoning," Orin Fletcher told her. "Will you trust yourself to me, Thankful?"

She nodded without even wondering why he drove up to the entrance of the City Hospital. He disappeared inside and came back at once with a little deformed man who had deep kind eyes. Behind them two men carried a great tank which they lifted into the rumble seat.

"Dr. Dean," Orin said abruptly, "he's going out with us. He's good with pneumonia."

Thankful wanted to tell him that it was too late, that they wouldn't have sent for her if—but there were no words to tell him. She listened absently to their talk together about their class at college, about their work, about—they were suddenly at the dock.

"Any way to get the cutter?" she heard the doctor ask, and hope lifted her heart faintly. That would mean Dave. Dave would help.

"Nothing doing," the agent said. "Off for a couple of days down east."

"Then get us the next fastest boat you can hire." Dr. Dean, so small, so crooked, reached up and laid a magic card on the shelf of the window which held the agent's indifferent face. The man clambered from his stool and stood in the office door. "Where to?" he said, and Dr. Dean was little and crooked no longer, in his eyes.

"Bright Island. And I'll need two men to load the oxygen tank."

In five minutes they were slipping smoothly, competently, through the crowded harbor, down past the lighthouse at its entrance, straight out to sea. Thankful could dimly remember the lift of spirit which the cutter's swift flight had given her. Now each muscle in her body pushed invisibly with the engines of this boat, urging it on. It was so slow! It was so slow!

Yet suddenly, as if she had pushed harder than she meant, the great white boulders of Bright Island gleamed at her. She turned, frightened, distraught, toward the two men still talking together in the stern. The deep eyes of the doctor met her and gave her their quiet. She looked back at her island. So it had always stood when she came, invincible, unchanging; so it would always stand. They belonged to it for a little while and then they left it. Gramp had left it, and now her mother—but shaking fear had taken itself away and left her with grief which could somehow be borne.

Jed's boat, her father's boat, swung at their moorings in the cove. The house looked empty and still except for white curtains blowing at her mother's windows. Did that room still hold her? Or was she gone, gone like Gramp? Her father stumbled down the beach like an old man and pushed out toward them in his peapod. She was shocked when she saw his face, hollow-cheeked, hollow-eyed, almost as if he had died too. She knew when he looked at her that hope had left him.

He accepted the two men with her, mechanically explaining in dull apology that Jed's boat was needed for the doctor, and he, himself, could not leave his wife. He did not even ask what was in the great tank when he helped to lift it.

"You are willing that I should consult with your doctor?" Dr. Dean asked him gently. Thankful's heart was wrung at his hopeless consent. But at least her mother was still alive.

They left the tank in the peapod. "I'd like to talk with your doctor first," Dr. Dean said. Old Dr. Black, fussing around the kitchen, was inclined to be testy with the crooked-shouldered invader. Ethel, swollen-eyed, large with dignity, stood by him.

"We got no right to trouble her anymore," she quavered. "She's asleep now and when she wakes—" She ended with a loud sob.

Thankful shut the kitchen door and gripped the knob hard. "This isn't for you to decide, Ethel." Her eyes smoldered under black brows like her grandfather, and Ethel shuddered. "My father has given his consent."

"Tut, tut." Dr. Dean touched her arm. "Where could we consult together, Dr. Black?" and the old doctor led the way to Mary Curtis's room.

After a few minutes Jed and his father went down to the

shore for the oxygen tank. The murmur of voices ceased. The two men returned and sat down in the kitchen where Ethel sobbed over a pan of frying fish. Thankful felt sick. The terror was coming back again. She looked desperately at Orin Fletcher, drawn into his corner as if he felt himself alien. He rose and with a gentle arm drew her out of the smoky kitchen.

"We'll not go out of hearing," he reassured her.

They sat down on a silver smooth log rolled up by the tide, and waited. Orin kept his arm about her and she rested in its comfort. The day seemed to be waiting for the turn of the tide, as she was. She quieted with it. Here on the island it was still winter bare. Yet there was warmth on the dead brown grass, and down at the tide edge the sandpipers were talking sweetly together. The high sun felt warm on her hands.

By and by a little deformed man sat there beside them and talked gently to them. He could not tell yet how things would go. Her mother was conscious. She had responded well. If they could keep her another twelve hours—he rose to go back to the house. "I will stay until then," he said, and Thankful thought she had never seen anything so beautiful as the smile in his deep eyes.

Somehow the day went by. The boys coming and going and finally staying, tiptoeing clumsily, talking in gruff whispers. Dr. Black said that he felt he could leave the case safely with Dr. Dean, and Jed took him back to the mainland. The little deformed man stayed with Mary Curtis. She put her hand in his, and they fought together.

At midnight they won. Her skin was moist and cool, her lungs breathed gratefully, she slept. And in her dreams she had once more toiled that rocky slope of Scotland, and once more could look down upon that fair country from its height, and realize its name, *Rest-And-Be-Thankful*.

She sighed in her sleep, opened her eyes and said, "I want to see my baby," and looked faintly surprised when Thankful knelt beside her. Then she smiled as if she saw a joke on herself, and slept again.

At dawn the doctor left, and all the boys, and Ethel. "She must be quiet with her home in its usual order." By now they trusted the crooked little man. He held them all in the palm of his strong-fingered hand. "I'll take Fletcher with me to bring back some things for her. He may stay on a few days? I'd feel safer. I'll come for him Sunday and look the patient over."

They were gone, all of them. Thankful turned from the departing boats and saw her island brightening in the dawn. Quiet, unchanging, patient as eternity. Her body felt light and her heart sang while tears rained down her uplifted face.

All day she moved about the house wondering at the ease with which she did her mother's tasks. I don't know how I know, she thought, but I do. Her mother's eyes, wasted, sunken, followed her, and once Thankful thought she heard a faint chuckle. Mostly she slept. Jonathan, wrecked like a mighty ship on the shoals of suffering, could not be persuaded to leave her to Thankful. But he lay on the couch with the old gray shawl across his tired hands and slept, too. Thankful gave him food as she would give it to a child, persuasively. When he ate irritably she was satisfied.

She pieced together the broken bits of things he told her into some sort of understanding of what had happened to her mother. Ethel had persuaded her to come over for the night. The children were getting over influenza and she didn't like to leave them for a church social she had promised to run. "Your mother'd been meaning to go over anyway to get me some new shirts"—from his haggard look she knew that in some obscure way he blamed himself. They had been hung up in a fog on the way back while he tinkered with dirt in the feed pipe which he should have cleaned out long ago. He noticed her teeth were chattering but thought she'd warm up as soon as they got home. And then he'd forgotten to put wood on the fire and the house was cold as the grave. Cold as the grave, he shuddered.

Thankful comforted him. "We islanders are tough," she said, "but we're not used to germs. They got her but they couldn't keep her down. Not with the care you took of her."

Jonathan eased gratefully back on the couch and slept again.

Late in the afternoon the big boat slowed into the cove, dropped Orin with his parcels, and moved smoothly away. Thankful rowed out to meet him, exulting in the hard pull of her muscles, flinging herself at the oars. How could she make him know what he had done for her? How could she make tangible this gratitude which flooded all her thoughts? She had no words to tell him or Dr. Dean. She felt that if she could catch handfuls of the lovely sunset light and hold them out to him, he would know how her life seemed to her now. She faced the radiant sky rowing him in, a dark figure in the stern.

"Are you," he said, "the same person I left this morning?" And even in the shadow she could see that the day had left its ravages upon him, and felt guilty at her own high heart.

"You shall have a good hot supper," she said because she could think of practical words only, "and then go to bed. I have your room all ready."

Thankful did not undress that night. She settled in the deep chair by her mother's bed, winding the alarm for a faint click when it was time for medicine. The night light shone dimly through her fair hair nodding over a book when Orin stole in at midnight to relieve her. They whispered together, conspirators for the quiet figure asleep. Thankful was to come again for him at four. Turnabout was only fair. He made her believe it in her weariness.

At four o'clock the household was plunged in deep

sleep. All except Orin Fletcher who dared not trust the click of a clock and paced softly, plunging his sleep-numbed face under the icy pump, until the dark house grayed before the still distant morning. Then he knew that he could let Thankful sleep no longer. He stood a moment over the old couch watching her, lashes dark against her cheek, breathing softly under the old patch-work quilt. She looked so pale, so young, in the thin light of dawn. His fingers touched the shimmer of her hair on the cushion and she was instantly awake.

"Is she worse?"

He shook his head and held her frightened hands. It was hard to talk. Then she saw the windows squaring themselves against the sky. She flung off the comforter and was on her feet all in one swift motion.

"You let me sleep! Oh, Orin, and you so tired!" She caught a frightened breath. "She *is* all right? She isn't worse?"

"Slept like a baby. Better than most." Her relief dazzled him. "Tell you what," he said, "let's have a cup of coffee and a snack before I turn in. I have a hunch I'm going to stay asleep once I get started."

On tiptoe they crept into the kitchen and shut themselves off with closed doors. The fire had kept well under Orin's stoking, and with open drafts the kettle began its tune. The smell of the coffee made them realize how inadequate toast would be. Thankful brought up eggs and a ham which swung in the cellar. Orin pared off thin slices which he would not allow Thankful to cook. He had a high opinion of his own skill. They ate at the kitchen table by the window in the first golden gleams of the sun. Outside an island robin sang, ecstatic over his return. Orin's eyes grew heavier over his last cup of coffee and Thankful sent him off to bed.

Mary Curtis opened her eyes when Thankful bent over her. "A bit of that ham I smell," she said, "and an egg. I'd like it fine!" She made a face at the cup of gruel which Thankful brought her and asked who the young man was who walked the floor all night. She seemed satisfied with Thankful's account, grinned when Jonathan poked his sleep-ridden face into the room, and slept again. Mary Curtis was on the mend.

Thankful carried the household as if it were a feather on her shoulder. The life which had poured back into Mary Curtis seemed in its abundance to have overflowed into her daughter. Its zest drove her, light-footed, over the beach like a sandpiper. It brought her back to her mother's room with gifts of sun and air. It filled her to the brim until her cup overflowed.

And Orin, when he found her after his long sleep, gathering sea moss for her mother, shared her heady wine. She had not meant to move him so deeply. She had not thought about him at all. Only of her own fullness of sweet new life, which could breathe and laugh and run swiftly.

He pulled her down beside him on the silver gray log where they had waited to know if death was victor. She was fragrant with the freshness of island air and Easter sunshine. Her lips which had been so tense in the grim wait, relaxed into warm curves. She was love, and laughter, and beauty, and all the glory which Orin Fletcher desired.

"Thankful," he said, "I love you," and his saturnine mouth worked as if like a child he realized how inadequate his words might be. "Wait," he said, "don't speak. I'll never manage to tell you again. You and I, we are one when we are together. We would always be. Think of the days in old Dinkle's boat. And deeper down, the way you are with me in my work, in our books together. Yes, I know that is all fun," he put in hastily, "but this hasn't been. Oh, Thankful, we've stood together these days. I've known your every breath."

He stopped but Thankful could not speak. Tears rimmed her lids with silver. Her throat was thick with them.

His tone lightened when he looked at her. "Don't do that," he said. "It's just that I'm hard put to it to know how to do without you when I go back today. And I'm harder put to it to see how I'd manage for the rest of my life. We could have a better time than most, Thankful." He sounded wistful in spite of himself. "I'm going back to Oxford for another degree next year. You'd like it over there."

Thankful shook her head and the tears dropped, crystal round on her hands. "I belong here," was all she could say. But she thought, he is so kind, so wise. I would like England. I could never, never follow him around while he lived his life. I belong here. This is my own life, here on Bright Island. Here I know how to live it. She looked pitifully at his eagerness and wished that she could tell him.

"Never mind," he said and rose at the shattering of their silence. Around the point swept the thin gray shape of the government cutter. "Doc got it this time," he said and started down the beach to greet it.

Thankful stumbled to her feet as if the tide had washed over her and left her unexpectedly breathing air again. Dave had come! Bringing the doctor! Oh, Dave! Dave! Everything would be all right now! And she flew to the house to have dinner for them, forgetting in youth's implacable way that everything had been made all right by someone else. That dark figure bending over the oars to bring the two men in to her.

To the Lee of Bright Island

The warm May sunshine poured over Thankful, and the cool May air blew against her face and ruffled her hair. Couldn't be better for drying paint, she thought, and drew slow competent strokes across the keel of her boat. The clean smell of wet paint, the new color under her brush, the feel of the boat's sweet curves, all part of a

May morning high and blue over her head, green and soft under her feet.

Where had the days gone, she thought, that it was May and her boat still on the ways? But she laid the paint on with unhurried satisfaction. The days were full, but time stretched ahead, time undisturbed by dread when it had run its course. A song sparrow in the alders scattered its melody like handfuls of silver, and Thankful's heart sang with him. Full of cares, and yet carefree, like him, she thought. For the cares were their own, of their own choice.

She heard the chug of her father's boat and knew that it was nearly noon and the potatoes must go on. She would go, yet the brush swept its bright track over and over until she heard his step behind her. She laid it on the grass and rubbed her fingers on some dry wisps before she reached for the mail which Jonathan had brought.

"Looks pretty fair," he conceded. "Needs a mite more by the rudder." He dipped the brush into the paint pot. "Want I should finish it for you?"

Thankful backed away, watched him grudgingly.

"Might get her off at full tide tomorrow if she's dry," he offered. "I'm kinda hungry."

Thankful yielded. Up on the bank among the pungent bayberries she looked back at the little boat, straight-masted, shining white in the sun. "Not too much of that copper paint," she called and felt as if she had done what she could for it. She ran swiftly toward the house where wood smoke already rose from the chimney.

Mary Curtis rocked comfortably by the window. "Get your boat done?" she asked.

"Almost. You built up that fire!"

Her mother looked over the mail which Thankful dropped on the table.

"Tillie-vallie!" said Mary Curtis. "If I can't feed the fire with a few birch sticks—" She ripped the wrapper from the newspaper and rocked and read.

Thankful moved about the kitchen unaware that her mother now and then peered around the paper's edge at her. What she saw evidently satisfied her. She went on reading. "You take hold pretty well," she said as if she read it out of the paper.

Thankful scarcely heard her. Swift, light, intent, she was as surprised as her mother when she stopped to think about it. Something in her must have watched alertly how things were done, must have busily stored its scrutiny for her use when she needed it. The Mary Curtis in her, perhaps, biding her time until she was needed. Gramp must share his kingdom with her now.

The hash was browning in the oven, the table was set, there was no further reason for delay. Thankful reluctantly pulled out from the mail a long school-stamped envelope. Now her mother openly watched her, dark-browed, anxious, bending over the typed paper.

"How'd you come out, lass?" but she knew because Thankful chuckled.

"They think I'm a whole lot smarter than you do." Thankful passed her the list of marks.

"Better'n you deserve," grumbled Mary Curtis. "That school doesn't know what scholarship is. Good mind to send them my judgment."

Thankful grinned. To please her mother, who had been deeply troubled because a girl should finish what she began, she had taken the final examinations. Orin Fletcher had sent them to her, and her mother had given them to her, and marked her severely when they were finished. Thankful had scarcely dared send them back to school. Now she felt extraordinarily lighthearted. The year finished, and finished well enough. Now it was off her mind. She would think no more about it.

She opened Orin Fletcher's letter while her father scrubbed the paint from his hands. And knew as she read it that you could not cut off a year of time like a yard of tape and discard it. It had woven itself into you and you would have to give it consideration always. Orin was sailing in one week, and under that statement she read his undefeated hope that she would join him. Oxford. His career. And a bitter sentence about the futility of tying herself down to such a limited life. My marks mean to him, she decided, that he made a right choice. And then was sorry. Because she remembered his dark suffering eyes when he said good-bye to her the day that Dave came.

She thought of Dave, and Orin Fletcher was a shadowy third. She recalled, if you could recall something so pervading that it made her day's plans, that Dave would be here before supper. And the shadowy Orin dimmed, faded into the folded letter. Thankful put the hash on the table and suggested that she take the powerboat over after Dave since her father had made the trip once today. Jonathan agreed and helped himself largely.

"Finished up your boat." His hunger seemed continually trying to repair the ravages of those days which had so nearly wrecked him. "Dave can help you get it off tomorrow. He'll be here the rest of the week, won't he?"

Thankful agreed with a high heart. "Once I get my hand on that tiller," she gloated, "Dave can be a passenger for once!"

"Dave's nobody's passenger," said Mary Curtis unexpectedly.

Thankful wondered what she meant, and said, "He's going to be mine."

"Dave'll have as much time for sailing as you will, my girl." Her father cut himself a huge piece of dried apple pie. "We finish getting that garden in while he's here. Ground's dry enough for the small seeds now." He tested the pie. "Not as good as your mother's yet."

Thankful agreed, but her mother flared. "Why would it be? Is nothing to be gained in thirty years of baking?

Suits me," and she ate a piece of valiant size. "Save the rest for Dave. He'll like it."

"Like it myself," grumbled Jonathan. "Not many ever could make pies like yours," and everybody was appeased.

"Doesn't seem right to make him work at planting when he has so small a time between jobs," Mary Curtis fretted. But she worried less as she grew stronger.

"He likes it." Jonathan pushed back his chair. "Spoiled a good farmer when they made a sailor out of that boy. Ought to be both, b'God!"

Thankful piled the dishes with a small secret smile. Might be yet, she thought.

"You, too, my lass"—Mary Curtis rested on the old lounge while Thankful washed the dishes—"from one thing to another the whole day through. You'll be worn down to the bone."

Thankful shook the suds from her hands and faced her mother. "I look it, don't I?"

Still in her overalls because there was Dave to get in the boat, sleeves high over smooth brown arms, yet in some strange way, more a girl because of the rough clothes of a man. "I'd no longer take you for an underfed boy, it's true," Mary Curtis admitted, and sighed as one does over the fulfillment of beauty.

A fresh southerly wind raced behind the powerboat all the way across. It would be wet charging back into it. Thankful hoped that Dave had sense enough to wear his oilskins. And a sweater under them. The softness of the spring air had sharpened into a crisp wind that bit like the salty edges of the waves. Yet there was still spring's promise in the high blue of the sky, in the beat of the sun. A few gulls soared airward as if for the pleasure of it. Fleetingly she missed her own gull. She thought, He's gone housekeeping on Gull Island as a gull should. He'll be back when it's cold. And fell to thinking of next winter and winters to come. Until when Dave stood leaning against a wharf post he seemed only to have stepped out of her thoughts.

She shut off the engine and held the boat still at the slippery ladder. Dave towered above her, buttoned into a new uniform which, Thankful admitted, did set him off. He made no motion toward the ladder.

"You won't look like that when you land," she observed.

"Well, how do I look now?" Dave asked.

"Pretty good," she said judiciously, and her eyes traveled up the brass buttons to his sunburned face. He looked excited, gay.

"All right, that'll do for now," he said and disappeared into the wharf shed.

Thankful swung at the ladder rail and felt warm happiness flow through her. As if the spring sun were liquid in her veins. The water was quiet under the pier and green. Sea anemones feathered along its piles. A carved sculpin traveled into its shadow. The dank seaweed under her hands smelled of the ocean which had left it. The boat swayed with her gently through a moment which seemed to hold her suspended, like a crystal drop in the deep pool.

Then Dave was beside her on the deck in island clothes and slicker. He stowed a neat leather case forward, and Thankful knew that her mother was also to have the treat of that new uniform. Then he took the wheel and not until they came in sight of the rocks of Bright Island did Thankful realize that he had not even asked for it. She hoped no one would notice who brought it up to the mooring.

Dave was huge and splendid in his uniform again at supper. He spoke largely of his new job, and under the shelter of its importance something young and anxious peered out to see how they took it. Just as if he had been their own boy, not intending to spoil him. Jonathan told him about the good farmer wasted, and Mary Curtis said the sea could yield as good a living as the land if you had the wit to handle it, which quieted Jonathan. Thankful sat in the shadow, and by the time the lamp was lighted they talked of other things.

At five the house stirred, but now Mary Curtis listened to kitchen sounds and Thankful made them. Only wet prints across the floor gave witness of an earlier icy plunge. Dave shook his head at them. He had seen her running through the morning light, but he had no words to speak of the beauty of that flying form.

Now she set hot muffins before him and he wondered when she had found time to bake them. "Good," Jonathan said. "Taste like that recipe of your mother's." Dave ate four of them. Thankful poured the bacon fat from the frying pan and wished for the smell of the clean black mould waiting to hold the seeds in its warm furrows. Planting was better than housework, she thought, keeping the muffins hot for her mother's late breakfast, but you couldn't do both. And there was her boat to be launched in the afternoon. The sun poured into the kitchen and she thought, it needs fresh paint, too. I'll get it on before Selina comes. Or better, she decided, Selina and I will do it together. It'll be a change from Bar Harbor for her.

The tide crept up the beach all day until it touched the beach peas and slid under the ways. A full moon tide. Thankful and Dave sat on the silver gray spar where she had waited in anguish so short a time ago, but now the pain was healed and the dark face comforting her shadowy beyond recollection. Later she would remember, but her own tide was at its full now.

When the highest reach of the water had wet the ways, they would launch their boat together and sail awhile in the quickened afternoon wind. They sat there in the sun with the fragrance of sweet fern about them, unhurried as the tide. Whitethroats whistled as if the world had just begun. They talked about Dave and his great boat, and Thankful laid a hand on her own small boat and remembered faintly the old promise to Gramp about marrying the sea captain, and the cruise over the world, and the little sailors growing up on Bright Island.

She had no sense of making a decision, but rather of flowing into a great river where all along she had been headed. An inevitable merging. Not a limited life as she saw it. She felt it whole and rich while they waited, the rhythm of the seasons with hard work and much beauty, the sea around her always, life and death in simple terms as she wanted them. Dave was an essential part of it all, strong to uphold her, dear to love her. She was content, and in the fullness of time would, like Mary Curtis, Rest-And-Be-Thankful.

About the Author

In 1951, Mabel L. Robinson wrote: "I went to normal school, taught a while, went to Radcliffe College, and finally took my master's and doctor's degrees at Columbia University, where I now teach creative writing. During the process of getting degrees I taught at Wellesley and at Constantinople College, where I taught many nationalities a great variety of subjects. On the side I had a great deal of fun.

"I live in New York, spending my weekends at our house in Montrose, a place which the birds have taken over, accepting me because I am a good provider. The four summer months are for Maine, where I have leisure to write, to sail, and to do as I please. It sounds very pleasant. And it is!"

Mabel L. Robinson won two Newbery Honors: for *Bright Island* in 1938, and for *Runner of the Mountain Tops* in 1940. She died in 1962.